Hubbard swam on the surface for fifty yards, very quietly towing the plastic bags behind him. He went under the boat, found the propeller shaft, and quickly tied everything in place. The last step was uncoiling the wire he had rigged between the detonators and the CB radio as he carefully rose to the surface for the last time. As soon as the CB radio was switched on . . . all hell would break loose on the ocean floor!

THE DEEP KILL

JACK DUGAN

CHARTER BOOKS, NEW YORK

THE DEEP KILL was written on a Lanier
"Super No Problem"™ Word Processor
Maintained By Joe Steele

THE DEEP KILL

A Charter Book / published by arrangement with
the author

PRINTING HISTORY
Charter Original / January 1984

ISBN: 0-441-14224-9

Charter Books are published by The Berkley Publishing Group,
200 Madison Avenue, New York, N.Y. 10016.
PRINTED IN THE UNITED STATES OF AMERICA

CHAPTER

1

Laura Wood got out of the chair in front of the television, pulled her sweater over her head, slipped out of her skirt, and walked across the elegantly furnished hotel room to the closet. She was wearing only a brassiere and panty hose. She was a slender, long-legged woman with broad shoulders and firm breasts. She wore a brassiere not because she required the support but because she thought there was something not quite decent about putting her nipples on public display. She took a black dress from the closet and pulled it over her head. She grimaced as she wrestled with the zipper, and then she smoothed the fabric down over her hips.

The telephone on the bedside table rang precisely at ten. Laura had left a call for ten. She didn't think it would be necessary or expect that she would fall asleep in the chair facing the television, but she didn't want to take that chance. She knew that she was exhausted mentally and physically, and it was better to leave the call than run the risk of waking up the next morning having missed her chance.

"Madam left a call for ten," the operator said. Very formal, very dignified, in keeping with the traditions and elegance of New Orleans's renowned Hotel Fairmount.

"Thank you," Laura said.

She slipped her feet into shoes and then returned to the bathroom, where she gave her dark brown hair a half dozen brush strokes and examined her pale lipstick, the only makeup she wore. Her skin was lightly and uniformly tanned, the skin of a woman who lived where there was a lot of sun and where one spent more time getting out of it than cultivating a tan. Then she picked up her purse, looked around the room, and walked out.

There were half a dozen taxicabs in line at the door of the Fairmount. A doorman whistled one up for her and put out his hand as he held the door for her. She gave him a dollar, not because she thought opening a taxicab door was worth a dollar but because she didn't have any change.

"Caroline's," she said to the driver. "It's a bar in the French Quarter. Do you know it?"

The cab driver snorted. "Yeah," he said. "I know it."

He didn't say anything else until they had crossed Canal Street and entered onto Rue Burgundy. They had gone two blocks before getting stalled in the heavy traffic on the narrow street. Then he turned around and looked at her.

"You must be new," he said. "I know most of the ladies who go to Caroline's."

"I'm new," she said, hoping it was too dark for him to see whether she was flushing. It was easier to let him think what he wanted than to go into a denial, which he probably wouldn't believe anyway, or tell him that she was going to Caroline's on business. Anyway, she thought with a little smile, that was probably what the ladies who frequented Caroline's Bar said, that they were "on business."

"Well," he said, "it should be a good night. There's supposed to be twenty-six hundred lawyers in town. Lawyers generally like a good time, and I never met a lawyer who couldn't afford what he wanted."

He was not, Laura understood, being nasty. He had simply and understandably mistaken her for someone else in the business of entertaining conventioneers.

"Let's hope so," she said.

Ten minutes and no more than a quarter of a mile later, the cab pulled to the curb in front of a four-story building on Rue Royal. She handed him four dollar bills for the three dollar and a quarter ride and got out.

"Have a good night," the cab driver said. "Good luck."

She found herself almost bumping into a cast-iron pole, one of a half dozen that supported a balcony over the sidewalk. She could hear a piano and a woman singing inside the building, but louvered blinds over the ten-foot-tall French windows kept her from seeing inside.

She saw a wrought-iron gate that when closed would effectively bar entrance to the brick building. On the wall beside the gate was a polished brass plaque. On one line it said "CAROLINE'S BAR" on the line below, "Opens 8:30."

That obviously means eight-thirty at night, Laura decided. Caroline's Bar, to judge from its reputation and what she could see of it from the outside now, did not look like the kind of place that opened for business early in the morning.

She walked through the wrought-iron gate and found herself inside a small vestibule. There was a huge, tall door in front of her with a polished brass plate on it. She pushed it open, grunting with the effort.

Immediately inside, slumped low in a leather upholstered armchair was an enormous black man in a dinner jacket. His head was shaved, and his very deep black skin seemed to glisten in the dim light. He was a bouncer, Laura understood, probably a very effective one. He was not the sort of man anyone sober or even someone very drunk would wish to challenge.

He was examining her, she realized, and very carefully. Then he nodded and smiled, exposing a mouthful of pure white teeth, and inclined his head toward the inside of the building, giving her permission to enter. I have just been examined, Laura realized, by someone who is qualified. I am now allowed to ply my trade at Caroline's Bar.

"I'm looking for Jack Hubbard," Laura said to the black man.

"Who?"

"Jack Hubbard," Laura repeated.

"Never heard of him," the black man said. "Sorry. You sure you got the right place?"

She knew that she had the right place and that the man was lying. She had sent Jack Hubbard a Christmas card. She had addressed the card to Jack Hubbard in care of Caroline's Bar. The black man was lying to her. She wondered why, and then she wondered why she was not surprised.

"Then I'd like to see Caroline," Laura said.

"She generally comes in some time during the night," the enormous black man said. "But you never can be sure. If I were you, I'd try to call, say, after ten tomorrow."

"I'll take my chances," Laura said.

She pushed open the heavy door and walked inside. Immediately to her left was a door leading to a crowded barroom dimly lit by a chandelier that must, she realized, be an antique and worth a fortune. There were probably a hundred faintly glowing bulbs. On the far side of the room was a piano bar, crowded with well-dressed men listening to an obese, deep-voiced woman playing and singing "Frankie and Johnny."

Laura thought that the prosperous-looking men were probably the conventioneering lawyers the cab driver had told her were in town. There were women among them, well-turned-out women, smiling brightly and being courted. They didn't look like what Laura thought high-class hookers should look like, and then she thought that maybe that was the definition of high-class hookers, that they didn't look the part.

Across from the piano bar was the bar itself, a long, old-fashioned mahogany bar with a brass rail. Behind the bar was an awesome display of liquor bottles. There were four bartenders in white jackets and an empty stool.

Laura made for the empty and sat down. She looked around for someone who could be Caroline. She realized that she was looking for a stout, silver-haired matron in an evening dress, covered with jewelry. The truth was that she had no idea what any madam would really look like, much less Caroline.

A pleasant-looking, rather muscular young bartender with long and carefully tended hair came to her immediately.

"Yes, ma'am?"

"I'd like to see Caroline," Laura said.

"Maybe she'll be in after a while," the bartender said. "No telling. Can I get you something to drink?"

"Scotch," Laura said. She had remembered hearing somewhere the rules of a place like this. When a man asked to buy them a drink, they ordered scotch or something else expensive and were served cold tea. Later, accounts were settled, with the price of the drink paid for being split between the bartender and the girl.

"Straight up? On the rocks? Soda? Water?" the bartender inquired.

"Straight up," Laura said.

The drink was promptly served, two inches of light brown liquid in a small glass. For appearances' sake, Laura took a sip. In the belief that she was getting tea, she took a healthy swallow. The raw scotch burned her mouth and throat, and she coughed.

"You wanted it that way, lady," the bartender said, amused. Then he asked, "You want me to put some soda in the rest?"

"Please," Laura said, pushing the glass across the bar.

The bartender took the glass, dumped the contents into a large glass, and added ice and then soda from a bottle of soda rather than a rubber hose device. Then he set the glass and the bottle of soda before her.

"I really want to see Jack Hubbard," Laura said to the bartender.

"He's not here," the bartender said. He did not deny that there was such a person, and Laura was encouraged.

"I thought Caroline could put me in touch with him," Laura said, and then added, "I'm running an errand for my husband. He and Jack are friends."

Laura thought she saw understanding in the bartender's eyes. If she was the wife of a friend of Jack Hubbard's, that would explain what she was doing there and even why she had taken a healthy swallow of the straight scotch.

"She doesn't know you?" he asked, making it a statement of fact.

Laura shook her head no. "Is there some way I could call her?"

He shrugged his shoulders in a gesture of helplessness. "All I can suggest is that you stick around until she comes in," he said. "Excuse me."

"Thank you," Laura said. She took a sip of her drink. She became aware that a man was smiling at her. She looked away. In a moment, the bartender was leaning over to her.

"That gentleman wishes to buy you a drink," he said.

"No, thank you," Laura replied.

The bartender nodded. "That's what I told him," he said, smiling at her.

That's even nicer, Laura thought. The bartender, who really knows about this sort of thing, knows that I'm not a hooker looking for business.

Laura smiled at him and told him thanks.

There was a mirror behind the array of bottles behind the bar, and Laura learned that she could look into it and see what was going on at the bar. She had never been in a place like this before. What surprised her most was that the hookers didn't look like hookers. She had expected that they would look tough, or worn, or sad, or brazen. But they didn't. They looked like average young women, except that they were better looking and better dressed than most young women.

"You wanted to see me?" a voice said in Laura's ear, startling her. She snapped her head around and found herself looking at a red-headed woman who didn't seem to be over thirty. She was dressed very much as Laura was, in a simple black dress and a string of pearls.

"You're Caroline?"

"Guilty," the redhead said. "Who are you, and what can I do for you?"

"I'm trying to get in touch with Jack Hubbard," Laura told her.

"He's not here, I'm afraid."

"Do you know how I can get in touch with him?"

"That depends," Caroline said.

"On what?"

"On what you want to see him for."

"I need his help," Laura said. "Jack and my husband were friends."

"Who's your husband?" Caroline asked.

"Art—Arthur—Wood," Laura said.

Caroline shook her head. "The name rings no bells," she said. The implication was that she knew all of Hubbard's friends.

"Have you got a telephone number you could give me?"

"What kind of help do you need from Jack?" Caroline asked instead of responding to Laura's question.

"I'd rather tell that to Jack," Laura said.

"Does Jack know you?"

Laura was tempted to lie but decided that that would be a mistake.

"He knows about me," she said. "You know, Christmas cards, that sort of thing. What it is, is that we need a diving job done."

"What kind of a diving job?" Caroline asked.

"I'd rather talk to Jack about that." She was afraid that saying that would anger this woman, but it did not. Caroline simply nodded her head.

"If your husband knows Jack Hubbard," Caroline said, "then he knows he's very good. And that he's very expensive."

"Yes, I know."

"For all I know, honey," Caroline said, "your husband and Jack have been best buddies since kindergarten. On the other hand, Jack might not even know your husband. So I have to treat you like anybody else who walks in here asking to talk with Jack."

"I understand."

"The way it is," Caroline said, "is that Jack gets a thousand dollars up front for what he calls a consultation. All anybody gets for the thousand is the chance to make their offer. If he doesn't take it, he keeps the thousand. He takes about one job in maybe six or eight. Now if, as you say, your husband and Jack are friends, you'd get the money back. But I can't turn you loose on Jack without the thousand up front."

"I understand," Laura said. "When can I see him?"

"You got the thousand with you?"

"I've got a checkbook," Laura answered.

"Cash," Caroline said. "Jack insists on cash."

"I don't know where to cash a check here."

"Did you notice the man just inside the gate?" Caroline asked. "The large man?"

"Yes."

"He operates a check cashing service," Caroline informed her. "He charges ten percent."

"Ten percent?" Laura asked in disbelief.

"Sometimes he has collection expenses," Caroline replied.

Laura looked at Caroline in confusion.

"You came in here looking for Jack," Caroline said. "It's up to you."

When Laura went to the enormous black man with the shaven head at the door, he didn't seem at all surprised that he was being asked to cash a thousand-dollar check on a Florida bank written by a woman he had never seen before. He got out of the armchair and motioned for another man to take his place. The other man, who was white and had long, carefully arranged silver hair, was just about as large. He too wore a dinner jacket. They were equally menacing, Laura thought.

The black man took her to a tiny office, which could have been at one time a closet, off a passageway leading to the rear of Caroline's Bar. Laura saw that the bar actually had two bars, the one she'd been in and another, larger one in the rear of the building.

She was asked for and produced her driver's license and two national credit cards, exactly as if she were trying to cash at her neighborhood supermarket.

"You understand," he said, "there's a ten percent service charge."

"I understand," Laura said, and wrote out a check for eleven hundred dollars.

The black man took a file card from a tin file box and printed the credit card numbers onto it. Then he carefully copied down the number and her address from her driver's license. He took an alligator passport case from the inside pocket of his dinner jacket and removed a thin stack of money. He counted out ten new crisp hundred-dollar bills and handed them to her.

"I think you'll find that's correct," he said.

"Thank you."

"So far," the shaven-headed black man told her, "it's been a pleasure doing business with you."

Laura walked back to the bar, where Caroline was waiting for her. She handed her the ten hundred-dollar bills. Caroline fanned them between her thumb and index finger, counting them quickly.

"Where are you staying?" she asked.

"At the Fairmount."

"Mrs. Arthur Wood, right?"

"I'm registered as Laura Wood."

"If you don't hear anything by ten o'clock tomorrow morning," Caroline said, "come here." She gave Laura a smile and walked away.

Laura turned back to the bar. Her drink was still sitting there. She picked it up and sipped at it, wallowing in the idiocy of what she had done. She had just given a thousand dollars in cash to a woman she had never seen before, and she hadn't gotten a receipt. The woman could deny ever having seen her or ever having received any money from her. She had set herself up to be plucked like a pigeon, and she probably had been.

She told herself that what was done was done. She had done something desperate because she was desperate. If she had to do it all over again, she would. She picked up her glass again and drained it in a single gulp. Then she opened her purse, took out her wallet, and looked for the bartender.

"What do I owe you?" she asked.

"That was on the house, ma'am," the bartender said.

Laura tried to lay a dollar on the bar, but he smiled and pushed it back.

She got off her stool and walked through the throng of conventioneering lawyers and the hookers to the door.

"Good evening, Mrs. Wood," the shaven-headed black man said politely. "There's a car for you outside."

"I beg your pardon?"

The large white man who had taken the large black man's place in the armchair by the door took her arm politely.

"Right this way, Mrs. Wood," he said. A black limousine sat at the curb, the door already open.

"Mrs. Wood is going to the Fairmount, Douglas," he said to the driver. He held her arm until she was in the car, and then he closed the door for her. The engine of the limousine started, and the car pulled away from the curb and began to move through the hordes of people who filled the street.

CHAPTER

Jack Hubbard sat slumped in a rubber-footed canvas and stainless-steel deck chair on the rear deck of the *Barbara-Ann*, a forty-two-foot sail-assisted trawler. His feet were stretched out before him nearly horizontally and were resting on the padded cushions of a large ice chest. He was a deeply tanned man of thirty-three, with a hundred and eighty-six pounds on his five foot eleven inch frame. His bare feet were stuck into a pair of canvas and rubber deck shoes. He wore underpants and a pair of faded, washed limp khaki pants. His lithely muscled chest was barely restrained by a brand new T-shirt on which was emblazoned "THE SEA WITCH BAR PASS CHRISTIAN, MISS."

The Sea Witch bar was owned by a retired Navy officer, a mustang who had worked his way up to commander before retiring. He and Jack Hubbard got along well. He had actually given Hubbard the T-shirt in a moment of beery generosity. Hubbard was not the kind of man to buy T-shirts with anything printed on them or wear them.

On Hubbard's wrist, nestling in hair bleached nearly blond by the sun, was a stainless-steel wristwatch on a stainless-steel band. The luminescent hands told him that it was nearly ten o'clock at night.

With him in the cockpit was a wiry little man of not quite forty years of age to whom the finance department of the U.S. Navy sent a monthly retirement check in appreciation of twenty years of service. He was Master Chief Diver Chester W. "Chet" Crawford, USN, Retired. Like Jack Hubbard, Chet Crawford held a can of beer in his hand and wore a bemused smile on his face.

They were watching a powerboat, large enough at forty-six feet to be honestly called a yacht, attempting with nothing coming close to success to back into a stall across the marina harbor from where they sat, bow in, in their stall.

They had just concluded between them several things. First, that the control problems the captain of the *Jo-Ann III* was having with his vessel were based on the fact that he was trying to navigate his twin-screw craft with one screw. The most difficult maneuver under that circumstance was backing. They had also concluded that the captain probably didn't know that.

It suddenly became too much for Chet Crawford to bear. He stood up, climbed onto the fish box, cupped his hands in front of his mouth, and bellowed, "*Nose* her in, asshole!"

It was the sort of thing that Chet Crawford had done during all of his career in the Navy, from the day he went aboard the Great Lakes Naval Training Station as a seaman recruit of seventeen until he retired, with an appropriate parade, at the U.S. Navy Underwater Warfare Laboratory at Panama City, Florida, in the Navy's highest enlisted grade. It was generally agreed by those who knew him, and by the Navy, that if he had been in the fleet or anywhere else but in Navy salvage, with his habit of calling things as he saw them, most often in a voice like a foghorn, Chet never would have been promoted above Seaman First.

But he had gone right from boot camp to diver's school and from diver's school to the salvage of a submarine that had gone down in three hundred feet off Massachusetts. He had come up from that dive with a Navy commendation medal and the beginning of the reputation that had followed him for the next twenty years: "Don't let the size of that little son of a bitch fool you; what he's missing in size he makes up for with brains and balls."

The yacht *Jo-Ann III*, which had been backing, reversed engines and stopped. Her master had heard the suggestion and, after considering it a moment, decided that it at least made more sense than what he was attempting. The *Jo-Ann III* began to move forward, making a sweep of the marina. A remotely controlled spotlight on her rigging above the flying bridge came on and, as she circled, searched the other yachts in the marina for the individual who had called out to her.

When the spotlight reached the cockpit of the *Barbara-Ann*, Chet Crawford stood up on the fish box, placed his left hand on the biceps of his right arm, and raised the right balled fist, center finger extended, in a sort of salute.

The spotlight died, a white light fading through a red glow to blackness.

"With your usual luck," Jack Hubbard said to Chet Crawford, "that guy is going to be six feet five, three hundred pounds, and mean."

Crawford jumped from the fish box to the walkway beside the *Barbara-Ann*.

"Where are you going?"

"If he was on one engine, something is probably wrong with the other one," Crawford said. "I need the money."

After his retirement from the Navy, and with the proceeds of a legendary poker game, Chet Crawford had bought a run-down boat yard on the Mississippi below New Orleans, which he had renamed Crawford Marine Enterprises, Ltd. He thought "Ltd." had a certain class. The boat yard, like its owner, had a fine reputation among the owners and operators of the boats that plied the Gulf, fishermen and work boats serving the off shore rigs. He did good work, and he did it cheaply, which meant that he frequently ran out of money and often turned up to see his old buddy Jack Hubbard to touch him for five thousand, seventy-five hundred, or whatever it would take to keep his head above water until the next check came in.

He had come to the marina of the Tidewater Beach Hotel, where Hubbard kept the *Barbara-Ann*, to put the touch on him for five thousand. Ordinarily this would have posed no problem, for Hubbard usually had money and was in the habit of lending it to Crawford whenever he needed it. But Crawford was third in line that week to put the touch on Hubbard. Hubbard's sister Margaret had called collect from Sioux Falls to tell him that her husband had been put on indefinite furlough by the company for which he worked as a mechanic. That had cost him twenty-five hundred, a loan that would be repaid within twenty-four hours of the Second Coming. Margaret's call had been followed three hours later by a call from Hubbard's older brother, Charley, in Cedar Rapids, Iowa, who reported that the goddamn diesel in the goddamn combine had thrown a goddamn rod and that it would take twenty-three hundred to get the goddamn thing running again.

That loan would be repaid within ninety days, with interest, if Charley had to hire himself and his boys, Hubbard's nephews, out as day laborers on the county roads. But when Hubbard had taken the forty-eight hundred from the strongbox under his bed to wire it to South Dakota and Iowa, there hadn't been much left, no more than two thousand.

That meant he was going to have to put the touch on someone himself so that he could give Chet his five thousand. The only person in the world who would lend Jack Hubbard five thousand dollars without security was his business partner, Caroline Dawson, and Jack Hubbard was the kind of man who hated to have to ask a woman for money.

"Let's hope that there's something really expensive wrong with it," Jack Hubbard said. He tossed his beer can in a precise arc into a plastic bucket, got out of the deck chair, jumped onto the walkway, and followed Chet Crawford down it.

Crawford had driven over from Louisiana in his truck, a ten-year-old panel. It looked as if it had given ten years of hard and faithful service and was six months from its deserved rest in a junkyard. In fact, it had been resurrected from a junkyard, and its running gear had been overhauled. On its muddy tires it could, and often did, cruise effortlessly at eighty-five miles an hour, while the driver, his tail cradled on foam-rubber-supported leather seats salvaged from a Cadillac Eldorado, listened to cassette recordings of Dixieland music through a 50-watt per channel stereo system, one ear cocked for the beep-beep-beep that came when his multichannel police radar detector was activated.

Crawford pulled the driver's door of the panel truck open and got behind the wheel. On the door was stenciled "CRAWFORD MARINE SERVICES LTD. BOAT BUILDING AND REPAIR. UNDERWATER WORK OF ALL KINDS. POINTE DE COCHON, LA." Hubbard got in the other side, immediately reached a hand out to shut off the stereo system, which Crawford rarely turned off and generally played very loudly, and then closed the door after himself.

The marina of the Tidewater Beach Hotel was laid out in an oblong, with the long sides parallel to the beach. A pier from the beach provided access to the stalls. An opening on the Gulf side of the marina gave access to the Gulf. The *Barbara-Ann*'s stall was on the opposite side of the opening to the Gulf, and so Crawford had to practically circle the marina to get to the stall where the captain of the *Jo-Ann III* was attempting to dock his vessel.

The *Jo-Ann III*'s captain had trouble getting it where he wanted it, even heading it bow in, but finally, with Hubbard and Crawford standing on the walkways on either side of the yacht and pushing it in place, they got her tied up.

The captain, instead of being six foot five and three hundred pounds, was more on the order of five foot seven and one hundred ninety pounds. He suffered from male baldness syndrome, the symptoms of which he attempted to conceal by parting his hair over his left ear and combing it over his skull to the right ear. However successful this arrangement might have been in an office, it failed rather pathetically while the captain was attempting to navigate his vessel in a fairly strong wind on one engine.

He jumped down from the deck of the *Jo-Ann III* onto the walkway, where he immediately encountered Chet Crawford's extended hand.

"Good job," Chet said enthusiastically. "Handling a ship that large on one engine is what separates the men from the boys, Captain."

If the captain recognized Chet Crawford as the man who had given him the finger five minutes before, he said nothing.

"Thank you," he said. "I lost an engine out there."

"Did you?" Chet Crawford asked sympathetically.

A dark-haired woman in her late twenties climbed onto the walkway and made her way to them. She was wearing a pair of tight-fitting slacks, deck shoes, and a white shirt through which her brassiere could be clearly seen and the tails of which she had tied in a knot below the swell of her bosom so that the tanned skin of her stomach was exposed to the elements. She also was wearing a wedding ring and a diamond engagement ring. The emerald-cut diamond was, Hubbard thought, at least three carats, maybe more.

Hubbard was leaning against the fender of Chet Crawford's truck. He felt her eyes on him as he examined her.

"Thanks for the help in tying me up," the man said, and then he nodded toward the truck. "That yours?"

Crawford nodded.

"I think I lost a propeller," the captain said. "What would you charge me to have a look at it?"

"Well, if you want to do it at my yard," Crawford said, "I'll haul her out of the water on the marine railway for a dollar a foot and have a look at no charge. But we're obviously not at the yard."

"I mean," the man said impatiently, "here and now."

"That poses a couple of problems," Crawford said. "For one thing, I'm not supposed to work on boats here."

"You were working on his, weren't you?" the man said impatiently, gesturing toward Hubbard. Hubbard, amused by Crawford's pitch, realized that the man had noticed the *Barbara-Ann* at her pier.

"He's got you there, Crawford," he said.

The woman smiled at him.

"Well," Crawford said easily. "That's a little different. Mr. Hubbard and I work together sometimes— we're divers—and I wasn't going to send him a bill."

"Look, let's stop the fencing," the man said impatiently. "Here's my problem. I'm going to entertain people aboard the *Jo-Ann* tomorrow. Customers, important customers. We came out here today to make sure that everything was all right, and then this happened. I'll pay you your regular charge plus twenty percent just to look at what's wrong and tell me whether I can use the boat tomorrow or not."

With reluctance in his voice, Chet Crawford said, "I have to charge a hundred an hour, two hundred minimum, whenever I go down. I mean, I got to have the tanks charged if I'm only down five minutes, and I really don't—"

"OK," the man interrupted. "Now we're talking business." He reached in his pocket and came up with a money clip. He peeled off two hundred-dollar bills and two twenties and handed them to Crawford.

"All right," Crawford said to him. "But I can't give you a receipt. You understand that? I mean, I'm really, if somebody should ask, not doing this for you."

"I understand, I understand," the man said. "Now will you have a look at it?"

"You want to give me a hand, Jack?" Crawford asked.

"Sure," Hubbard said.

He walked to the back of the truck and opened the door. There were two sets of self-contained underwater breathing apparatus strapped to racks mounted against the side of the truck. He took one of them, checked it to make sure there was air in the tank, and then carried it to the walkway and handed it to Crawford. Then he returned to the truck and came back with two waterproof battery-powered lanterns. By that time, Crawford had strapped the yellow scuba gear onto his back and was checking its operation.

"You want to turn your back, honey?" Crawford asked.

"That's Mrs. Fortin," the *Jo-Ann III*'s owner said sharply.

"I'm about to take my pants off," Crawford replied. "I thought I should warn her."

"You want to go in the cabin, Jo-Ann?" the man asked.

Crawford unzipped his pants and stepped out of them. He laid them on a fighting chair, picked up one of the lanterns, stepped onto the railing, and simply stepped over the side. There was a splash, and he disappeared.

"We seem to have forgotten the amenities," Jo-Ann said, stepping to Hubbard's side and putting her hand out to him. "We're the Fortins. I'm Jo-Ann, and that's Harry."

Her hand was warm and soft in Hubbard's. Harry Fortin's hand was soft and somewhat clammy.

"Jack Hubbard," he said.

"I've admired your boat," Harry Fortin said, and then he got to the point. "Is he any good? Does he know what he's doing?"

"They don't come any better," Hubbard said. "You're lucky he was here."

"You in business together?" Fortin asked.

"We work together sometimes," Hubbard said. "I'm in the marine salvage business." He didn't like Fortin's implication, and it showed in his voice.

"Let me get you something to drink," Jo-Ann Fortin said. "What'll it be?"

"Sour-mash bourbon if you have it."

"Coming right up," Jo-Ann Fortin announced. She disappeared into the cabin.

"What exactly is marine salvage?" Harry Fortin asked.

"When people lose things underwater," Hubbard explained, "I try to get them back for them."

"That sounds very interesting," Mrs. Fortin said from inside the cabin.

"I read somewhere," Fortin said, "that if you find something at sea, it's yours. I guess you could make a pretty good buck that way."

"Sometimes," Hubbard agreed. "And sometimes not."

"I'm in the truck leasing business," Fortin offered.

"I guess you could make a pretty good buck that way," Hubbard said, making a gesture around the *Jo-Ann III*.

Jo-Ann Fortin appeared with drinks. When she handed Hubbard his glass, her fingers brushed his longer than necessary. He looked into her eyes and then walked to the stern and looked over the side. There was a faint glow to indicate that somebody was down there with a bright light, but that was all he could see.

Chet Crawford stayed down ten minutes, and then his head appeared at the swim platform. He rested his elbows on it, took the mouthpiece from his mouth, and called up to Hubbard.

"I think you'd better come down and have a look for yourself," he said.

"I'd rather not," Hubbard said.

"Please, Jack," Crawford said. "I can't handle this by myself."

Fortin winced. That announcement was going to cost him money.

"Oh, all right," Hubbard said. He went to the truck and got the second scuba and another lantern. When he returned to the *Jo-Ann III*, he strapped the equipment on, tested it, and then turned to Jo-Ann Fortin.

"It's pants-off time again, Mrs. Fortin," he said.

"Oh, please call me Jo-Ann," she said, and walked toward the cabin.

Hubbard slipped out of the khaki trousers. Then he climbed over the aft railing and started down the stainless-steel ladder to the swim platform. He glanced at the cabin door. Jo-Ann Fortin was standing just inside, looking at him. There was a faint smile on her face, and as she let her eyes drop from his face down over his chest to his jockey shorts, the tip of her tongue came out between her lips.

Hubbard went down to the swim platform and then slipped into the water. Crawford had gone under first. Hubbard swam to Crawford's light. What was wrong with the starboard engine of the *Jo-Ann III* was immediately apparent. It was the practice of both the deep water and the coastwise freighters that called at Gulfport to carry deck cargo and cover it with sheets of heavy plastic. Despite Coast Guard regulations specifically prohibiting the practice, it was their habit to remove the plastic when they had just about made port and throw it over the side. Sometimes the long sheets of heavy plastic sank immediately in the channel, and sometimes air caught in the folds kept the plastic either afloat or floating around just beneath the surface.

The *Jo-Ann III* had run over a sheet of plastic and wrapped it around her starboard propeller. The effect of a sheet of plastic around a propeller was to put frightening vibrations into the prop, driveshaft, and engine. Hubbard took a quick look at the plastic and then shined his lantern on his face and shook his head, signifying understanding.

Crawford held his fist in front of his face and opened the fingers, made another fist, and then opened them again. A thousand dollars.

Hubbard shook his head and held up five fingers. Five hundred was more than enough. Crawford signaled seven hundred. Hubbard flashed five again. Crawford reluctantly signaled OK with his head and pushed himself back toward the stern of the yacht. Hubbard followed him.

When he climbed up the ladder to the cockpit, he saw that Jo-Ann Fortin was again in the cabin and again looking. Why not? Hubbard thought. Wet T-shirt contents were very popular.

"Well, what do you think?" Harry Fortin asked.

"It looks like you ran over something out there," Crawford said.

"I know that," Fortin said. "What I'm asking is, can you fix it?"

"I think so. It'll take two, three hours. Two of us times three hours at a hundred an hour is six hundred dollars. So I'll tell you what I'll do. Call it five, and I'll have you ready to run at eight o'clock in the morning."

"I'm insured," Fortin said. "For five hundred bucks,

I'd like to submit a claim."

"Then you'll have to get somebody else," Crawford said. "I'm not licensed to work here."

"Oh, to hell with it," Fortin said. "I'll make it up someplace." A shrewd look appeared on his face. "I'll leave my wife here, and the minute you get it running, I mean, show her it's running right, she'll give you another two hundred and sixty dollars. You won't mind staying over, honey, will you?"

"If you think I should, dear," she said. "If you think it's necessary."

"If something goes wrong—no offense, Crawford— and it's not ready by eight o'clock in the morning, you call me, and I'll think of something else to entertain those people."

"All right," she said.

"We better get to work," Crawford said, putting the scuba mouthpiece in his mouth again. He stepped to the railing and jumped in the water. Hubbard this time jumped into the water too.

It took them about fifteen minutes to free the propeller from the plastic sheeting tightly wrapped around it and its shaft. It had to be cut, and it was for all practical purposes nearly invisible in the water. Then, in silent agreement, towing sheets of the plastic behind them, they swam underwater across the marina harbor to the *Barbara-Ann*. Hubbard climbed out of the water first and then reached down to take the heavy plastic from Crawford. He carried it to a fifty-five-gallon waste barrel on the pier and jammed it inside. Then he went aboard the *Barbara-Ann* and took a long hot shower.

He dressed in fresh khakis and a T-shirt without a legend and then went into the cabin. Crawford had just about finished cleaning the scuba gear.

"That was a quick five hundred, wasn't it?" Crawford asked.

"I'll go get the balance owed," Hubbard said.

"I figured you would, you bastard," Crawford said.

"If you had listened to your sixth grade teacher, who told you that smoking cigarettes would stunt your growth, you too would be tall, handsome, and irresistible," Hubbard said.

"Screw you, Jack."

The car that had been on the pier by the *Jo-Ann III* was gone when Hubbard walked around the marina to the yacht. Jo-Ann was in the cabin.

"All fixed," he said. "I gather that Mr. Fortin has gone back to New Orleans?"

"Uh, huh," she said. "It took you longer than I thought it would."

"I'm sorry to have kept you waiting."

"It's all right," she said. "Where's your friend?"

"Taking a shower."

"And you've already had one, haven't you?"

"Uh huh."

"Pity," she said. "I was thinking we could have taken one together."

"They say you never can get too clean," Hubbard told her.

"Oh, we'll think of something else interesting to do to one another," she said, and took his hand and led him through the cabin of the *Jo-Ann III* into the master stateroom, where the bed was already turned down and there was a bottle of sour-mash bourbon and two glasses sitting on the bedside table.

CHAPTER

3

The telephone was ringing when Chet Crawford came out of the *Barbara-Ann*'s shower. He hesitated to answer it. There were very few people who had the Biloxi marina telephone number, and one of them was Caroline. He did not like the idea of talking to Caroline, because then he would have to deal with the problem of why she couldn't talk to Jack.

But it would be worse not to answer the telephone. If it was something important and Caroline couldn't get an answer, she probably would get into the limousine and come over. It was only an hour's drive from the French Quarter to the marina. It was better to answer the telephone.

"Hello?"

"Who's that?" Caroline demanded suspiciously.

"Crawford."

"I didn't know you were with him," Caroline said. "Let me talk to him."

"Can't."

"Where is he?"

"Comforting an unsatisfied wife," Crawford told her. "Where else?"

"Very funny, Chet."

"Cross my heart and hope to die," Crawford insisted.

"I don't suppose that I've got much of a chance to get him away from the game for a couple of minutes to talk to me, do I?"

"I can try, Caroline," Crawford said.

"Is he winning?"

"No," Crawford said. "To tell you the truth, he's down a lot, nearly a thousand."

"Then I really don't want to disturb his concentration, do I?" Caroline said as if to herself.

"Not unless it's important."

"There was a woman in here a while ago, looking for him."

"I swear to you, Caroline," Crawford said righteously. "There's been no woman looking for him over here."

"I know, I know," she said impatiently. "She was here ten, fifteen minutes ago. She says her husband and Jack are friends."

"What's her name?"

"Her husband's name is Arthur Wood," Caroline said.

"Never heard of him."

"Neither have I," Caroline said. "But I think she's legitimate."

"Why do you say that?"

"Because when I asked her for a thousand dollars, she came right up with it."

"What does she want?"

"Some kind of diving job."

"I could go get Jack," Crawford said, "and have him call you back."

"No," Caroline said after a moment's hesitation.

"Just make sure he gets the message. She's going to be here at ten in the morning. If he wants to talk to her before then, she's at the Fairmount."

"The Fairmount?"

"I smell a lot of money here," Caroline said. "The Fairmount, for one thing. The way this one dresses, the way she talks. This one's a lady."

"So what do you want me to do?"

"Tell him what I told you," Caroline said. "Tell him that unless I hear from him, the woman will be here at ten in the morning."

"I'll go get him now if you like," Crawford offered again.

"Chet," Caroline said impatiently, "just tell him what I said." She hung up.

Laura Wood woke up at half past seven in the morning. The room was flooded with sunlight diffused by the drawn curtains. She knew that once she was awake, she could never go back to sleep. She had slept restlessly, troubled by dreams. As she rolled over onto her stomach, she remembered with mingled amusement and chagrin that one of her dreams had been erotic.

She had been in a hotel room in her dream, this room or one very much like it, with the very large man with the carefully combed silver hair who had been at the door to Caroline's Bar and had put her into the back seat of the limousine.

"Let's see what you got, honey," he had said to her.

She had protested.

"I paid good money to see it," the very large silver-haired man had replied.

That had seemed an irrefutable argument, and so she had showed it to him.

He had dropped to his knees and gone down on her.

She was, she told herself, your typically sexually frustrated widow, straight from a soap opera.

Then there had been something, she knew, about

being in Caroline's Bar, from the moment the cab driver here at the hotel had mistaken her for one of the hookers. When she actually had seen the hookers, and they hadn't appeared cheap or tawdry, she had very naturally wondered what it would be like to offer herself to a stranger for money. She'd had that fantasy from time to time since she had started thinking about sex.

And those men, both of them, the white one and the black one, had been so menacing.

She suddenly rolled back over onto her back and then sat up. Sex, she told herself, wasn't her problem. Getting Art's insurance was. She had had six thousand four hundred and eighty-six dollars, what was left from her parents' insurance, money Art hadn't known about. Counting the money from the sale of the house in which she had grown up and the insurance money, there had originally been close to two-hundred and forty thousand. Close to a quarter of a million dollars in other words. She had turned it all over to Art as a dutiful wife, and Art had promptly spent it. All that was left of the money was the house and the airplane.

They had paid cash for the house, but then, later, Art had talked her into signing a mortgage on it. She didn't understand why they needed the money the mortgage brought. That was when she was pregnant and before she had learned that Art liked to run over to Daytona Beach, park the airplane, and bet large sums of money on the jai alai games. She never knew and didn't want to know what he did with the money he had won.

The Cessna was mortgaged too, and she'd signed that mortgage and was liable for it.

Both the house and the airplane had mortgage insurance. If she could prove Art was dead, the mortgages would be paid. If she couldn't, on the first of the month, when the airplane payment was due, they would start harassing her for the money or the plane, and she wouldn't have either. A couple of months after that, when the six thousand four hundred and eighty-six dollars was gone and she couldn't make the mortgage payment on the house, she and Little Art would be out on the street.

On welfare? Would it come to that? Would she become one of those women you saw on television standing in line for aid to dependent children? She had no skills. She couldn't even type or take shorthand. A degree from Vassar in medieval history wasn't worth a dime in the marketplace. It was probably worse than no education; she would be overqualified for a job as a cashier in the supermarket.

Maybe, she thought, she would wind up as a hooker. Maybe some of the women she had seen last night in Caroline's Bar had gone through something like what she was going through. If you have to sell something, she thought, you sell what you have.

She pulled her nightgown over her head, walked naked to the bathroom, and turned on the shower. The water was cold, and she let it run as she looked at herself in the mirror. Having Little Art hadn't ruined her figure. She still had that as a negotiable asset.

When steam began to fill the room and cloud her image in the mirror, she shook her head and told herself that her present line of thinking wasn't going to get her anywhere. She wasn't quite that desperate yet. There was still Hubbard.

She'd heard about Hubbard again from a Coast Guard chief petty officer. She'd first heard of him from Art. Hubbard, according to Art, was a powerful man who "owed him a big one." He had gone to New Orleans to see him, to make a deal with him. Art had never talked about it again, and so the deal, like so many of Art's deals, had more than likely fallen through.

But you can't live with a man and not learn about him. She sensed that this man Hubbard did in fact owe Art a "big one." She had learned to tell the difference between Art's wishful thinking and the truth. Hubbard, she believed, owed Art. Whether he would pay up was something she would just have to find out.

When she'd gotten word that the plane had gone down, the old Coast Guard chief petty officer, probably against the rules, had taken her out on the boat to the crash site. The cutter that normally would have gone out was busy chasing drug runners, and so the Coast Guard had sent the old chief out alone on a thirty-two-footer, half ship (there had been a machine gun under a tarpaulin on the foreward deck) and half pleasure boat. He'd felt sorry for her and hadn't had the heart to turn her down when she'd begged to go along.

She had been able to see on his face that he was genuinely sorry for her when he'd told her that the Coast Guard just didn't have the time or equipment to spend a lot of time looking for the airplane in forty feet of water off the Dry Tortugas, much less recovering a body from it. As cold-blooded as it sounded, the mission of the Coast Guard was to preserve life, not clean up after an accident, unless debris presented a hazard to navigation.

She was going to have to hire some salvage guy, he told her. They'd come out with a barge and some divers, and for a price they'd find the airplane and pick it up and do whatever she wanted with it.

"That's going to cost you plenty, I'm afraid," he said.

"And what if I don't have plenty?" she asked, forcing a smile, trying to make her voice a lot lighter than she felt.

"That's the way it is," he said gruffly. "I'm sorry."

Then he'd gone into the business with the map, making a copy of the first map he'd marked when they were out by Fort Jefferson in the Dry Tortugas. The marks showed the current and the wind and where they'd found the oil slick and the pieces of the plane that had floated to the surface.

"A chart like this is important," he said. "They don't like it unless it's neat and tidy." She hadn't understood him then; he'd practically had to spell it out for her.

"The only way you can get a chart like this from the Coast Guard," he said, "is when you present a license from the state of Florida to conduct an underwater salvage operation."

Then he had folded the chart neatly and wedged it against the windshield of the little boat.

"When we get back," he said, "I'll have to make sure to remember to destroy that. Unless the wind maybe blows it over the side."

She was sometimes very dense, but she wasn't that dense. When he excused himself to have a look at the engine, she put the chart in her purse.

He didn't seem to notice that the chart was gone when he came back. Maybe ten minutes later, he said, "There is one guy."

"What?"

"There's one guy who might be able to help you," he said. "Just *might*."

"I'm desperate."

"His name is Jack Hubbard," the Coast Guard chief had told her. Then he'd stopped. "Look, you didn't get this from me, OK? He's got a lot of people down on him. Nobody's proved anything on him, but he'd done time, and . . ."

"You mean he's been in prison?"

If he was a friend of Art's, that really wasn't at all surprising.

"Yeah. And I heard—I don't know, I heard—that they threw him out of the Navy. He used to be a chief warrant officer. He's not the kind of guy the Coast Guard approves of, if you know what I mean."

"But then, why?" Laura asked, leaving the sentence unfinished.

"I seen him work one time," the chief told her. He stopped. "You know, this is really none of my business."

"Please go on."

"I was stationed in Louisiana, and there was a fire on one of those offshore drilling rigs. Gas. The drill stem snapped, and the gas was just coming out of the ground into the water and then bubbling up, and when enough of it accumulated, it would get set off by the fire on the rig and then blow again. You understand what I'm telling you?"

"I think so."

"So all these high-priced oil guys are out there fucking—excuse me."

"It's all right."

"Well, all the experts were out there and getting nowhere, the gas kept coming up and blowing, and they finally were willing to try anything, so somebody sent for Hubbard. He told them he'd stop the blowout for five grand down and a hundred thousand when it was out. They were spending maybe thirty, forty thousand a day anyway, so another five was peanuts to them, so they told him to come ahead.

"He came out there on his boat. He's got one of those Fiberglas cruising trawlers."

"Excuse me?"

"They're sort of copies, Fiberglas, of the Grand Banks Trawlers. All plushed up, of course, but the same hull. Good boats. They're rigged for sail, and they can go anywhere."

She had no idea what he was talking about, but she asked no more questions. She was sorry she had interrupted him at all.

"Anyway," the old chief went on, "he had it loaded down with three hundred pounds of composition C3, which is a plastic explosive, and as much pig iron as it would carry and one other guy, and some scuba gear."

"Scuba?"

"Air tanks, diving gear. It stands for self-contained underwater breathing apparatus."

"Oh, yes."

"So he chases everybody else away, and he and this

pal of his go into the water, and they're down there maybe an hour, and then they come up and get in the boat, and maybe ninety seconds later there's this big explosion and a great big ball of fire in the air, and everybody figured he'd screwed up and damned near got himself killed. But that was it. Nobody knows how he did it, but he blew that hole closed. No more gas escaped. The fire went out and stayed out, and he collected one hundred thousand for a day's work.''

''You think he'd be willing to help me?'' Laura had asked.

''No,'' the chief had said. ''I mean, I wouldn't count on it. What I was doing was just thinking off the top of my head. What I'm saying is there's two ways to get what you need done. One is hire one of those marine salvage firms. They'd come out here with a barge and spend a week, two weeks, three weeks, at say three thousand, thirty-five hundred a day, and they'd eventually find the plane and get a cable on it and haul it up, and you'd have the plane and Mr. Wood's body.''

''What's the other way?'' Laura asked.

''Talk Jack Hubbard into getting what you need. He could go down with scuba gear, send the body up, blow the engine or the tail off, something to prove the plane was down there, and he'd probably do it for, say, twenty thousand.''

''I don't have twenty thousand dollars,'' Laura Wood had said.

''That's why I said I didn't think he would help you. You could offer him a down payment and a piece of the action, and if he wasn't busy and the idea appealed to him, he just might take you up. I don't think he would, but I thought I should tell you about him.''

''Where do I find him?'' Laura asked, feeling deceitful. She knew where to look for Jack Hubbard, at Caroline's Bar in the French Quarter in New Orleans. But she didn't want this decent, kindly old man to know that her husband knew him.

The old chief looked deeply embarrassed.

"That's another reason a lot of people don't like him," he said. "He's sort of in business with a woman named Caroline. I don't suppose you've ever heard of Caroline's Bar."

"No." Laura had lied, and she felt badly about it.

"You want me to stop beating around the bush?" the old chief asked.

"Please," Laura said.

"If you want to get in touch with Jack Hubbard, you can find him at Caroline's Bar. If he's not there, Caroline, who is either his girl friend or not, will know where he is. It's in the French Quarter," he said. "It's supposed to be the oldest fancy house in New Orleans. Hubbard's supposed to own half of it."

"I see," Laura said primly. This Jack Hubbard person seemed like an altogether splendid human being. He had been thrown out of the Navy, had been in prison, and owned a whorehouse. Just the kind of man Art would admire and be proud to have in his debt.

Laura did not shrink from calling a whorehouse a whorehouse. She was facing facts, and the fact that mattered most of all was that she was going to be out on the street unless this man Hubbard could be persuaded to help her.

She had tried to call him as soon as she was back in Fort Myers and had quickly learned that Jack Hubbard was a hard man to find. The three people who had answered her three calls to Caroline's Bar denied ever having heard of him. Then she had done the only thing she could do. She had left Little Art with Mrs. Newton next door and caught a plane to New Orleans.

As she showered in her hotel room, she thought that it was entirely likely that there would be no telephone call this morning from either Caroline or Jack Hubbard and that when she went to Caroline's Bar, it would be closed. Nobody there would remember ever having seen her or her thousand dollars.

She got dressed and wondered what to do about breakfast. She didn't want to pay what the Fairmount wanted for room service breakfast. She had made reservations at the Fairmount because that's where her mother and father had always stayed. As disturbed as she was, it had slipped her mind that she was in no position to spend money like they had. But if she left the room, there might be a telephone call.

She solved the problem by staying in the room and not eating. The phone did not ring.

At half past nine, she tried to call Caroline's Bar. The phone rang and rang, but there was no answer. She decided to walk from the Fairmount to Caroline's Bar. That should, she thought, kill the time between now and ten o'clock, which was when Caroline, probably laughing at her gullibility, had told her to come.

The French Quarter looked much different in the daylight than it had the previous evening. Some of the people on the streets were obviously conventioneers, but they were no longer traveling in hordes. An army of street cleaners and garbage men were cleaning up the previous evening's debris. The doors to the striptease joints were open, and she saw people inside cleaning them up for the next night's business.

When she got to Caroline's Bar, she saw with surprise that it was within a stone's throw of St. Louis's Cathedral. The building itself was larger than she had remembered, and it wasn't hard for her to imagine it as it had been in the middle of the nineteenth century. It had been a mansion then, and horses had been tied to the cast-iron horse's head hitching posts in front of it.

Her heart sank, however, when she saw that both the door and the wrought-iron gate that guarded it were closed. There was a knocker on the gate, and so she worked it. It was ineffective. The wrought iron was thick with paint, and the knocker was stiff to move and made very little noise. She was about to quit, had just decided the only thing she could do was leave—coming back at night when the place was open obviously would be futile—when she saw a tiny door buzzer button set into the bricks of the archway. She pushed it and very faintly, far inside the building, heard the buzzer sound.

No one came for a long time. She pressed the buzzer again, figuring that while she very likely had seen the last of her thousand dollars, had been played for the gullible innocent that she was, she wasn't going to give up without a fight. Then the inner door opened. It was the silver-haired man of the night before, the one from her erotic dream. She felt her face color.

"I'd like to see Caroline, please," Laura said.

He didn't reply, but he came to the gate and put a key into a substantial lock and then pushed the gate outward to let her in. When she was inside the gate, he locked it carefully and then pushed past her into the building, holding the door open for her.

The room with the two bars and the beautiful chandelier where she had met Caroline was empty. It obviously had just been cleaned, and there was the pungent smell of a disinfectant in the air. She followed the very large man past the office where the very large black man had cashed her check, toward the rear of the building. He stopped before a door and unlocked it with another key from a full key ring. He pulled the door outward, and Laura saw that inside was an elevator. He stepped inside, put yet another key in a lock, and motioned her inside. The door closed. The large silver-haired man's cologne quickly filled the tiny elevator. The elevator moved slowly, and there was no sound.

"Hydraulic," the silver-haired man said. "Installed in 1889."

It took her a moment to figure out what he meant, and by then the door in front of her slid open.

"To your left," he said, motioning.

She was in a luxurious apartment. She realized after a moment, when she saw the furnishings, that it had not been decorated but re-created. This floor of this building was furnished as it must have been furnished in the last half of the nineteenth century. Except, she thought, for the stereo. There was the sound of music. She progressively identified it. Dixieland. Not New Orleans. New York. An old recording. Probably Eddie Condon.

She somehow knew that she was in Caroline's apartment, the apartment the madam shared with the ex-con she had to appeal to for help.

She moved down a corridor and came to the large room in the front of the building. The floor to ceiling windows were draped and had Venetian blinds. The blinds on one window were open, and she could see the spires of St. Louis's Cathedral and the trees in Jackson Square and the Calbida Apartments on either side of the square and beyond that a huge freighter making its way down the Mississippi River.

She was so startled by the beauty of that sight that it was a moment before she saw the man sitting at a table to one side of the room, sitting so that he could look out the window too.

"You're Mrs. Wood?" he asked.

"Yes," she said.

"This is yours," he said, and slid a piece of paper across the polished surface of the Louis XIV table at which he sat. Laura looked at the paper and then at the man in surprise. The paper was her check. This was obviously Jack Hubbard. Why was Jack Hubbard returning her money, including the hundred-dollar service charge?

CHAPTER

4

"Take it," Jack Hubbard said to the woman who had just entered Caroline's sitting room.

He pushed the check and the hundred-dollar bill another six inches across the table. She was a good-looking female, he thought: wholesome and vulnerable. She was not the sort of woman you thought of in connection with a man like Art Wood. But then he thought about it and realized that he was wrong. Art Wood was the kind of man who would have a wife like this. From the time he had been in high school, he had been aware of the perverse attraction of decent, wholesome women to miserable sons of bitches.

He wondered again why he had never gotten whole-some-looking women. The ones whom most other men found sexy turned him off, but the reverse was not true. As a general rule of thumb, decent, wholesome women showed no interest in him at all. Or, women he thought were wholesome and decent and who succumbed to his pursuit soon proved that they were neither wholesome nor decent. The absolute proof of that theory was Barbara-Ann.

Laura Wood walked across the floor onto the rug in front of the table. She leaned over and picked the check up.

"I do," he said, interrupting her. "But I owe your husband. I don't take money from people I owe."

"I do," he said, interupting her. "But I owe your husband. I don't take money from people I owe."

There was relief in her eyes when she looked at him. It wasn't hard to figure that out, he thought. Wood told her I owed him, and she hadn't believed him. She obviously had been married to Wood long enough to know about him.

"I'm having breakfast," Hubbard said. "Have you eaten? Can I offer you something to eat?"

"Oh, I don't—"

"Please," he said. "It's eggs creole," he said, lifting a silver plate cover and showing her. "Louise always makes too much."

Laura met his eyes. They were gray, she thought, and intelligent and penetrating, looking right into her—somehow menacing.

"I haven't had breakfast," Laura admitted.

"Then sit down and have some," he said, nodding his head toward a velvet upholstered chair, a twin to the one he was sitting in. He made no move to get it for her, and so she got it herself. He turned in his chair and without getting up pulled open a drawer in an antique, darkly gleaming cherry cabinet nine feet tall. He came out with a knife, fork, and spoon.

"You are Mr. Hubbard?" Laura asked.

"Jack Hubbard," he said. He got up, walked out of the room, and returned with a coffee cup and saucer.

"I can send for cream and sugar," he said.

"Black is fine."

"There's chicory in there," he told her. "Some people find it bitter."

"I'm sure it will be fine."

"Help yourself," he said, taking the silver plate cover off the eggs and setting it on the table.

The silver serving bowl, which Laura recognized as both sterling and almost certainly antique, contained a bed of chopped, sautéed vegetables and four poached eggs. She scooped some of the vegetables and a poached egg onto her plate and, after a moment's hesitation, a second poached egg. The truth was, she was starved.

"I don't know what this is," she said.

"Tomatoes, celery, onions, fresh parsley, garlic, and a little okra," he told her, "sautéed in a little garlic-flavored olive oil."

He picked up a long, light-green, thumb-thick cigar and lit it with a wooden match.

Laura sampled the vegetables. "It's very good," she said truthfully.

He thought that she really must be in love with her husband, be willing to do anything, whatever he wanted, for him. Coming here to Caroline's Bar twice took a lot of guts. Most middle-class or upper-middle-class women wouldn't have made it through the door the first time.

Caroline came into the room. She was wearing a pleated, lightly plaided skirt and a pale blue wool pull-over sweater. There was a string of pearls around her neck, and she was carrying a grocery bag. She took a jar of orange marmalade from the bag and set it on the table. She did not look like a madam is supposed to look, Laura thought. She looked like a suburban house-wife.

"Have a cup of coffee," Hubbard said to her. "I know you're curious."

"Good morning," Caroline said to Laura. She walked out of the room and returned in a moment with a cup and saucer. She sat down in another of the velvet upholstered chairs and sipped her coffee.

"Mrs. Wood was just about to tell me what errand

her husband has sent her on," Hubbard said.

"Art is dead, Mr. Hubbard," Laura said.

He looked at her a moment before asking in a level voice, "How did that happen?"

"He was killed in a plane crash."

"I'm sorry," Caroline said.

"When?" Hubbard asked.

"Three days ago," Laura said.

"Where?"

"Off Fort Jefferson, in the Dry Tortugas," Laura told him.

"And he gave you my name? In case you needed help?"

"He said you owed him," Laura said.

"I owed him," Hubbard said. "But I think you should know that I didn't like him."

"Jack, for God's sake," Caroline shouted. "You *are* an insensitive son of a bitch!"

"I didn't like him," Hubbard said. "And Mrs. Wood frankly doesn't strike me as your typically grief-stricken widow."

"I hated the son of a bitch," Laura said.

"In that case, Mrs. Wood, what can I do for you?" Hubbard asked.

"I need to get his body out of the airplane," Laura informed him.

"If you hated the son of a bitch," Hubbard said, quoting her, "then why don't you leave him where he is?"

"Jack, damn you!" Caroline said.

"I need the body to prove he's dead," Laura began.

Hubbard finished the sentence for her: "Because without a body, there's no insurance payoff."

"That's right. Not for seven years."

"You don't look like your typical greedy bitch, either," Hubbard said. "So there must be a kid."

"If I were a man," Caroline said. "I'd knock your . . ."

Laura nodded. "A boy," she said. "He's three."

"Tell me what happened to him," Hubbard said.

"Art ran a charter service," Laura began. "You knew that?"

"Yes. I knew that."

"Well, he was called out to a yacht in the Dry Tortugas. To pick up a passenger, maybe passengers, who wanted to return to Fort Myers."

"Or maybe ten pounds or so of cocaine?" Hubbard asked.

The accusation frightened Laura. It put into words that which she was afraid to think.

"I don't think so," she said.

"Why not?" he asked reasonably.

"He was going out to the *Non-Deductible*. That's Dexter Corten's yacht."

"Who is Dexter Corten?"

"He's a real estate developer," she said. "I just don't think he's the sort of man to be involved with drugs."

"Pillar of the community? That sort of thing?"

"Yes," Laura said.

"I'll let that ride," Hubbard said. "So what happened?"

"He crashed on landing."

"Whatever else he was," Hubbard said, "your husband was one hell of a pilot. What happened?"

"I don't know. The old chief—"

"Who?"

"The Coast Guard chief who went to the scene. He said the only thing he could figure was that the floats hit something in the water."

"Did he say why he thought that?"

"Because Mr. Corten told them that the float was torn off. The Coast Guard found that floating around."

"Just the one float?"

"Just the one," she said, looking at him and meeting his eyes.

She's uncomfortable, he thought, maybe even frightened. But not of me. Can she sense that my weak spot is women like her? He nodded, and she went on.

"And the plane sank immediately. Mr. Corten told the Coast Guard that it just went up on its nose and over on its back and sank."

"Sometimes," he said levelly, "a plane like that will float for an hour."

"He said it sank immediately," she said uncomfortably.

"Did he tell you that, or the Coast Guard?"

"I haven't seen him."

"Was he alone?" Hubbard asked. "Do you know if he was alone?"

"I drove him to the airport," she said. "He was alone."

"And now, to collect his insurance, you have to recover the body. And you've come to me for that. Is that about it?"

"Yes."

"Why me?" he asked. "There are marine salvage people in Fort Myers. And Marine Salvors in Key West are about the best in the business."

"I can't afford them," Laura said.

"What makes you think you can afford me?" Hubbard asked.

Caroline made a grunt of disgust.

"I'm willing to pay you for your services, Mr. Hubbard," she said.

"How?"

"From Art's insurance."

"How much insurance?" Hubbard demanded.

"Two hundred and fifty thousand dollars."

"With or without the double indemnity?"

"With it," she answered.

"Are you sure about the insurance?" Hubbard asked. "I mean, are you sure Art didn't cash the policy in?"

"I paid the premiums myself," Laura told him.

"The airplane was probably insured too, right?" Hubbard went on. She nodded. "And there will probably be some mortgage insurance payment too?"

"That's right," she said. "The mortgage on the house will be paid off."

"A Cessna on floats is worth, say, fifty thousand," he said. "What's your house worth?"

"We paid eighty-five thousand dollars for it."

"Call it ninety with inflation," he said. "Ninety plus fifty is a hundred and forty thousand. A hundred and forty and two hundred and fifty is three hundred and ninety thousand. With that kind of money down the pike, you shouldn't have any trouble getting a salvor to take a shot at it on speculation."

"The people I talked to want ten thousand dollars down," Laura said, "and thirty percent of my insurance payments."

"And you figured, since I owed your husband, that I would come a lot cheaper?"

She met his eyes. "Yes," she said. "I thought about that. I have to make do from now on on what's left."

"Plus Social Security," he said nastily.

"What the hell is the matter with you, Jack?" Caroline demanded.

"I suspect that the lady's husband was engaged in a business venture with swarthy Latin American types from, say, Colombia," Hubbard said. "And don't accuse me of being foolish. If a salvor wants thirty percent, that thought has crossed his mind, too."

"What makes you think my husband was involved with drugs?" Laura demanded.

"Because the last time he tried to call his IOU, that's what he had in mind for me," Hubbard said.

"Mr. Hubbard," Laura said, "if you're trying to get me to, I don't know, get hysterical and tell you to go to hell and run out of here, I won't."

He looked at her thoughtfully. "The people who deal

in drugs are very nasty people," he said. "By that I mean that they kill people. All the time. They scare hell out of me."

That was, she thought, a very unusual thing for someone like him to say.

"I don't know if he was involved in drugs," she said truthfully. "He may well have been. But I don't think so."

"The wife is often the last to know. So what it boils down to is that you're here calling his IOU, right?"

"That's what I'm doing," Laura said. "I'm the most ferocious and dangerous of animals, a mother protecting her young."

"Jack, that sounds exactly like something you would say," Caroline said, chuckling.

"I've thought about it," Laura said. "About Art being involved with drugs. If he had been, all along, I mean, there would have been a lot of money. There wasn't."

"How much money do you have?" he asked.

"A little over six thousand dollars."

"And you have to live, right?" he asked. "Food, shelter, whatever?"

"Yes, of course."

"For me to take my boat down there and do what has to be done would cost five thousand dollars," Hubbard said. "Minimum."

He looked at Caroline, who gave him a dirty look.

"As the tennis set would put it," Hubbard said to Caroline, "that puts the ball in your court."

Caroline looked at him without expression for a long moment, and then she glanced at Laura.

"I don't think there's that much in the house," she said. "I'll have to send somebody to the bank."

"Does that mean you'll do it?" Laura asked.

"I'll tell you something you can hear on any used car lot," Hubbard said. "Because I like you, and because it happens that I'm having a little cash flow problem, I can make you a deal you can't afford to turn down. What I'm prepared to do for you, for exactly what it costs me, payable if and when I'm able to recover your husband's body and an identifiable part of the aircraft so that you can collect his insurance, is go down there with you and look for the body for five days. I mean five days on the site, not five days total.''

"Thank you," Laura said.

"I always pay my debts," Hubbard said. "One way or the other."

He took the napkin from his lap, laid it on the table, and then stood up. "Let's see how Crawford feels about getting his throat cut," he said.

"You go ahead," Caroline said. "I'll see about getting you the money."

"Thank you for that," Laura said.

"No thanks necessary," Caroline said. "I'm sorry for you, but not five thousand bucks sorry. I'm loaning the money to him, not to you."

Laura felt her face flush. Then she followed Hubbard to the rear of the apartment, where a glassed-in sun porch offered a view of the French Quarter toward Rampart Street. There was a small bar built against the side wall, and on a stool before it sat a small, wiry man Laura had never seen before. He was drinking coffee from a mug. A restaurant-style glass coffeepot sat on the bar.

Laura remembered the old chief telling her that Hubbard had put out the gas fire in the Gulf of Mexico with a friend, and she decided that the small, wiry man was the friend.

"This is Mrs. Arthur Wood," Hubbard said. "I'm going to do a salvage job for her."

"Is that so?" Crawford asked.

"I'm going to recover her husband's body from a plane crash off Fort Jefferson in the Dry Tortugas," Hubbard said. "You interested?"

"Sure."

"There's no money in it," Hubbard told him. "I'm paying off a debt. You still interested?"

"Sure, Jack," Crawford said. "If you say so."

"Like hell you are," Hubbard said, chuckling.

"Hey, Jack," the small, wiry man said. "I owe you. If you're in, I'm in."

"Sure you are, Chet," Hubbard said. "Just checking."

"Shit," Crawford said.

"Is there anything that I should do before you can get down there?" Laura Wood asked.

"The first thing you do is make out a check for five thousand dollars," Hubbard said. "I wouldn't want you to forget that in your excitement if we should be able to recover the body."

She was surprised and hurt, and it showed on her face, for Hubbard swung around on the stool and looked at Laura out of his cold gray eyes.

"Let me tell you how it is, Mrs. Wood," he said. "You may be what you appear to be, a very nice lady with a very serious problem. On the other hand, you were married to Art Wood. You stayed married to Art Wood. That may be because you're overendowed with loyalty, or it may be because you were two of a kind. I have very uncomfortable feelings whenever anybody wants me to do something in the Dry Tortugas. Either I have the Coast Guard breathing down my back, or I have Spanish-speaking people trying to cut my throat."

"I'll give you a check," Laura said, taking out her purse.

"This won't get cashed unless I recover the body," he said as she was writing out the check.

"Since we are being so frank," Laura said as she tore the check from her book, "how do I know that?"

He chuckled. "You don't have to worry about that. From now until I'm finished with this job, you and I are going to be closer than newlyweds on their wedding night."

"I don't understand," Laura said.

"It's very simple," he said. "If I'm either going to jail or going to get my throat cut, I'm not going to be alone. This is your operation, and you're going to be in on it from start to finish."

Laura met his eyes. "I'm in your hands, Mr. Hubbard," she said, handing him the check.

"As the fly said to the spider," Caroline said a trifle nastily as she came onto the sun porch.

Laura looked at her and then back at Hubbard.

Hubbard endorsed the check to Caroline and handed it to her. "This is to be cashed in the event I get the body," he said. "Or on the day you hold my memorial service."

"Don't be funny, Jack," Caroline said.

"I'm not being funny at all," he insisted. "If I get blown away doing this, Art Wood and I are square. Then it's cash on the barrelhead for services rendered."

"I don't understand that," Laura said.

"Your husband once saved my life," Hubbard said. "At the risk of his own. I'm now repaying that debt. If I get killed trying, I have a large family who can use that five thousand dollars."

"What happens now?" Caroline asked after a pause.

"Chet goes back to Boloxi and has a look at my engines," Hubbard said. "Then I go with Mrs. Wood while she checks out of her hotel. And then Mrs. Wood and I go to Schwegeman's."

"Who's Schwegeman?" Laura asked. Maybe, she thought, Schwegeman was the friend the chief had talked about and the small man was somebody else.

"It's a supermarket," Hubbard told her.

CHAPTER
5

Schwegeman's turned out to be the largest super-market Laura had ever seen, covering an entire block under the I-10 bridge in East New Orleans. They drove there in Hubbard's car, a three-year-old station wagon. The car didn't appear to have been washed since it was new, and the fenders and panels were dented and rusty.

"We'll need two," Hubbard said to her as they passed the line of shopping carts.

He jerked one apart from the others and started off. He did not offer to help her when she had trouble separating hers from the others, and by the time she got it free, he was out of sight. It took her a couple of minutes to find him. By then, his cart was half full of fresh vegetables and meat. When she caught up with him, he started putting groceries in her basket.

She had just decided that they looked like a young married couple doing the family's shopping for the week, when he bent over to get something from a bottom shelf and his left trouser leg was pulled up. There was a strange bulge inside his stocking, and then she recognized it for what it was. There was a .38 revolver in an ankle holster inside the stocking.

The gun disturbed her.

"I know I'm not supposed to ask questions," she said.

"But?"

"What are we doing with the groceries?"

"We're going to eat the groceries," he said. "We are going to put them on my boat, and we are going to cook them, and they are going to give us sustenance while we cruise the romantic Gulf of Mexico." His eyes were smiling at her. It was the first time that had happened.

"You can ask questions like that," he said. "I just don't want you questioning anything I do when we get where we're going."

"All right."

His last stop in Schwegeman's supermarket was the liquor department. He put four half gallons of Schwegeman's Private Stock 98 Proof Kentucky Sour Mash Bourbon into his cart and then loaded the bottom tray on his shopping cart and hers with four cases of beer.

Fear returned. She was going to be alone on a boat with two men for at least a couple of days, however long it took to get to the lower end of the Florida peninsula. If Hubbard came on to her, what could she do about it?

And with liquor in him, he might do just that.

She was a little surprised when she realized that what she was thinking was closer to wishful thinking than a bona fide fear of rape.

Chet Crawford was sitting in the cockpit of the *Barbara-Ann* when Hubbard and Laura Wood drove up in the station wagon. That identified him, Laura thought, more or less positively as the friend the Coast Guard chief had mentioned.

"There's a little problem come up," Crawford said by way of greeting.

"Don't tell me," Hubbard said. "You can't go."

"I got a chance to make a flying three thousand," Crawford said. "So what I figured was I could go back to the yard, do what has to be done, and then fly down to Florida."

"Don't bother, Chet," Hubbard said. "You do what you have to do. I can do this myself. Nobody's going to make any money on this operation."

"I got to figure it that way, Jack," Chet said.

"If I need you, I'll send for you. We'll leave it like that."

"Right. Yell and I'll come running," Crawford assured him.

Hubbard turned to Laura. "You can bring the groceries aboard," he said. "I'm going to check the gear."

She went to the station wagon, picked up two of the bags of groceries, and carried them on board the *Barbara-Ann*. She was surprised at the boat. She didn't know much about boats, and she had never seen one like this before. It was built of glistening white Fiberglas but still looked more like a fishing boat than anything else. There was a mast coming out the top of the cabin, and it was functional, for there was a furled sail on a horizontal cross-member.

The interior was comfortable, even a little plush. The cabin was roomier than she had expected. There was a galley with a refrigerator and a freezer, both of them larger than the freezer and refrigerator she had at home. Both were nearly empty, although the freezer held a good deal of frozen fish and fish bait.

There was a passageway three steps down from the cabin with doors opening off it. There was an array of controls and instruments and radio equipment against the forward wall of the cabin, with a swiveling stainless-steel, plastic-upholstered chair mounted before them. A stainless-steel ladder led to a hatch in the cabin ceiling, and she guessed that there were dual controls outside.

She wondered whether Hubbard had bought this yacht with his proceeds from marine salvage or his proceeds from his share of Caroline's Bar or some other shady source of income.

It took her five trips to carry the groceries aboard and a sixth trip to get her luggage from the station wagon. By the time she came aboard with her suitcase and overnight bag, the engines of the *Barbara-Ann* were running and the boat was trembling from their vibration.

Without asking her whether she was finished, Hubbard shouted to Crawford on the wharf to let loose the lines. Laura left her suitcases on the deck of the cabin, went out to the cockpit, and climbed an outside ladder to the deck over the cabin. There were, as she thought there would be, a dual set of controls under a white canvas Bimini top. As she walked to Hubbard, the boat began to move.

He glanced at her but said nothing as he carefully moved the *Barbara-Ann* out of its slip and then through the marina and finally out into the Gulf of Mexico. Crawford stood on the pier with his hands on his hips and watched them go, but neither he nor Hubbard waved or said anything to each other.

"You see that hatch on the deck, way forward?" Hubbard asked.

"Yes," she said when she located it.

"Go down there and stow the lines in it," he ordered. "And then stow the aft lines in the hatches you'll find there."

She did as she was told, and then she climbed back up to the deck over the cabin.

"I'd like to change clothes," she said, "and put my suitcases away. Where do I sleep?"

"Help yourself. There's only one cabin with a bed in it," he said.

She smiled at him and went below, wondering what he had meant by that remark. When she went looking for what she thought would be a guest cabin, she learned that he had meant it literally. There was only one cabin equipped with a bunk. The master's cabin was furnished comfortably if not plushly, with a full-sized double bed, a shower, and even a small couch. But when she opened the other doors in the passageway where the other cabins should be, she found them either empty of anything or crowded with equipment, air tanks, generators, and two deflated large rubber boats with outboard motors to propel them.

She obviously was expected to share the bed in the master's cabin. The question was whether she was expected to share it with him in it.

Laura changed out of her skirt and sweater into a knit shirt. She would have liked to wear a pair of shorts but decided against that and put on a pair of pants instead. Then she climbed up onto the deck over the cabin again.

"The answer is, we'll take turns in the bed," Jack Hubbard said to her, having read her mind. "So relax."

She didn't reply.

"You got the groceries put away?" he asked.

"Yes."

"You leave some steaks out?"

"Yes," she told him.

"Sit here," he said, getting up from the rubber-footed stainless-steel deck chair in which he had been sitting behind the wheel. He motioned her into it.

"This is our course," he said, pointing to the compass. "It's on autopilot, so all you have to do is sit here and make sure it doesn't vary more than a couple of degrees. If we come close to some other boat, give me a yell." He pointed to a microphone and switch marked "PA."

Hubbard went down the ladder. A moment or two later, she heard a sharp whistle. Startled, she turned around and saw that the hatch in the deck was open. Hubbard, in the cabin below, was looking up at her.

Then a bottle of beer came sailing up through the hatch. She caught it instinctively. Hubbard disappeared from sight.

Laura sat down again in the deck chair. She looked around. Biloxi already was fading on the horizon. She was out in the Gulf, alone with a man like Hubbard, far from any help if she needed any. Hubbard's friend Chet Crawford had made it plain that he thought they were on a wild goose chase.

Why then, Laura asked herself, was she experiencing this sensation of pleasure, of having no worries?

She stuck the neck of the beer bottle under her knit shirt, so that the cap wouldn't cut her hand and twisted it off. The beer was cold and good. It must have been on the boat already, for the beer they'd bought in the supermarket had been warm.

Was he trying to get her drunk?

Girls drank, she remembered hearing, because they could do things drunk that they couldn't do sober.

The truth of the matter, she told herself, was that Jack Hubbard really turned her on.

When Jack returned to the deck over the cabin of the *Barbara-Ann* twenty minutes later, he handed Laura Wood a sandwich unlike any she'd ever eaten. He had broiled one of the New York strip steaks and then sliced it very thinly. He had then laid the strips on a piece of the French bread he had bought in Schwegeman's and topped them with thinly sliced raw green bell pepper. Then he'd poured the pan juices over everything.

It was delicious, and she told him so. Then she added, "You're really quite a gourmet, aren't you?"

"I like to eat."

"Is it permitted for me to ask where we're headed?"

"Somewhat against my better judgment," he said, "we're going to fuel up at Panama City. It's about a thirteen-hour run. We should get there about two-thirty in the morning."

"Why against your better judgment?"

"Boats like this leaving Panama City have a nasty habit of disappearing," he said.

"Disappearing?"

"Pirates," he said. "The chamber of commerce doesn't like to hear that word, so they try to blame poor seamanship, and if that won't wash, they make vague references to the drug trade. But a pirate is defined as someone who diverts a vessel and/or its cargo to his use on the high seas by force."

Laura wasn't sure that she believed him. She was sure, however, that she didn't want to argue with him.

He changed the subject. "We're close enough to shore to pick up television," he said. "Mobile, then Pensacola, and finally Panama City. You have to aim the antenna. There's a chrome wheel in the overhead. Why don't you go watch TV?"

She would have preferred to stay where she was, but she didn't want to say so. She was afraid that he would interpret it as a statement that she wanted to be with him. She went below and after a little bit of trouble managed to get the antenna pointed at a Mobile, Alabama, television transmitter.

She arranged herself comfortably on a couch in the cabin and watched the tail end of a soap opera and then the first part of the evening news. Then she fell asleep.

It was dark when she woke up, and when she sat up on the couch, she could see electric lights, houses, and automobile headlights out the port windows of the cabin. She was a little stiff, and she shivered when she sat up. She went to the master's cabin and took a sweater from her suitcase before going out onto the deck.

She got there in time to hear him curse. She saw that they were close to a wharf with fuel pumps.

"What's the matter?" she asked.

He pointed to a sign announcing the hours the fuel point was open. It opened at 4 A.M.

"At least we'll be first in line," he said.

She put her wrist under a dull lamp glowing to illuminate the engine instruments on the control panel. It was a little after two.

"Well, you can take a nap," she said. "You must be tired."

He sighed. It made her want to slap his face.

"I don't suppose you know how to use a pistol?" he asked, his tone anticipating a negative reply. "Or a shotgun?"

"No," she confessed, shaking her head.

"Why don't you go make us some coffee and maybe a bacon and egg sandwich," he said.

It was an order, and she complied as he backed the *Barbara-Ann* away from the fueling wharf and then, going forward, moved two hundred yards away. She heard the rattle as he let loose the anchor, and then the engines died.

She thought that he would come into the cabin to eat the sandwich, but he didn't, and so she carried it up to him on the deck. It was dark, and it took her eyes a moment to adjust. When they had, she saw that the pistol holster he had strapped to his ankle was now on his belt and that there was a police-type riot shotgun laid across the arms of the deck chair.

"Go below and lock the cabin door," he said as he took the sandwich and coffee from her. "You take a nap."

"I slept all the way here."

"Do what I tell you," he said flatly.

Laura went down the ladder and into the cabin. The television was still on, but there was no picture. She shut it off and went back to the couch. She felt herself getting drowsy again, and although she fought it, she went back to sleep.

She woke when he started the engines. It was just getting light. She went back onto the deck over the cabin.

"Take the line out of its hatch," he ordered, "and

when we get into the dock, throw the end to the guy."
He pointed toward the dock, where a stocky young man
who needed a shave was waiting for them. She went
down the ladder and made her way to the forward deck.

The *Barbara-Ann* took on four hundred forty gallons
of diesel fuel.

"You were pretty dry, Captain, weren't you?" the
unshaven young man asked.

"It was a long way across the Gulf," Hubbard replied. "I had another couple of hours of fuel."

"Where you headed?" the young man asked.

"Mobile," Hubbard said matter-of-factly. "We're
out of Tampa for Mobile. I'm ferrying her."

"She's nice," the bearded man said.

Hubbard didn't reply to that. He took a leather wallet
from a cabinet in the cabin and paid for the gas in cash
from a stack of fifty-dollar bills.

Five minutes later, as the sun came up, they passed
under the harbor bridge and went back into the Gulf of
Mexico.

"Why did you tell him we were headed for Mobile?"
Laura asked.

"There's a slight chance that he just might believe
me," Hubbard said.

"I don't understand."

"You don't believe me about the pirates, do you?" he
asked.

"I don't know if I do or not," she admitted.

He shook his head. Arrogant goddamn male chauvinist, she thought angrily.

But doubt came when she saw that he actually headed
southwest, toward Mobile, until they were out of sight
of shore. Then he headed south-southeast, directly into
the open expanses of the Gulf.

He engaged the autopilot and turned the wheel over
to her.

"You can run it from here," he said. "Or if you get
cold, and sometimes it gets damned chilly out here, you

can go down in the cabin and use those controls.''

"It's nice now," she said.

"With any kind of luck at all," he said, "we should make Boca Grande Island in about twenty-six hours. All you have to do is sit here and keep your eye on the compass and give a yell if any boat comes within a mile or so. Or looks like it's headed for us. Then you come and wake me up. OK?"

"OK."

An hour or so later, Laura had to go to the toilet. It was a call of nature that could not be long denied. After thinking about it for a moment, she went quickly down the ladder and into the cabin. She had expected him to be in the bed in the master's cabin, but she found him asleep where he had been, on the couch in the cabin. There was an Army rifle with a large magazine for the cartridges sticking out the bottom on the deck beside him. He didn't wake up as she made her way through the cabin to the master's cabin, and she had almost made it back to the cockpit when he spoke.

"The next time you have to go to the head," he told her, "let me know."

She turned, flushing a little, and nodded her head.

"No need to be embarrassed," he said. "I have it on the highest authority that even the Queen of England has to tinkle from time to time."

He gave her a smile and then let himself fall back against the cushions of the couch.

Soon after that Laura got hungry, but she was reluctant to wake him again, and so she stayed where she was. The sun was fully up now, hidden from time to time behind clouds that appeared perfectly white against the solid blue of the sky. The surface of the Gulf was smooth, with large gentle swells. If not for the circumstances and Hubbard's melodramatic pirate business, it would be a very pleasant place to be.

By ten o'clock she was really hungry, and she wondered how long he would stay asleep on the couch. By ten-thirty she was more than a little annoyed with him. He had no right to just leave her up here without anything to eat while he slept in the cabin.

She looked around the empty surface of the Gulf, and just at the moment when she saw the boat almost straight ahead of them, two or maybe three miles away, she saw a flare arc into the sky from it.

A distress signal, she knew. The boat halfway from there to the horizon was in trouble.

She went down the ladder as quickly as she could and woke Hubbard up and told him what she had seen.

"Damn!" he said. He swung his feet off the couch, picked up the Army rifle, and climbed up onto the flying bridge. He opened a drawer in the control console and slipped the rifle into it. Then he took out a large pair of battered binoculars. When he put them to his eyes, she saw the legend on a brass plate fixed to one of the tubes: "US NAVY Binoculars, Commanders, 8×57."

She wondered if he had stolen them. The Coast Guard chief had told her that he had heard Hubbard had been kicked out of the Navy. He looked through the binoculars for a long moment and then took them from his eyes.

"May I?" she asked.

He handed her the binoculars. It took her a moment to find the boat on the horizon and another moment to focus. But then she could see the other boat quite clearly. It was another cabin cruiser about the size of the *Barbara-Ann*, and she could make out four people on it, four men standing on the deck, on the flying bridge, and in the cockpit, all of them waving their arms. Two of them waved towels or T-shirts or something white.

"I guess they're glad to see us," Laura said to Hubbard.

"You bet your sweet ass they are," he said. "We

might have really been on our way to Mobile.''

"You're not going to tell me you think they're pirates?"

"I'm not going to tell you a goddamn thing," he said. "Just shut up, Mrs. Wood, and let me think."

He took the binoculars from her again, stared through them at the other boat for a long time, and then turned. He went to the ladder, but instead of using the steps, he slid down to the deck on the stainless-steel handrail and then went into the cabin. Laura picked up the binoculars and looked again at the men waving to them from the obviously disabled cabin cruiser.

Then she heard Hubbard swear again, very bitterly. She looked down into the cockpit. When she didn't see him there, she looked over the side of the flying bridge. Hubbard was on the narrow strip of deck that ran along the outside of the cabin from the cockpit to the forward deck. He was holding a piece of wire in each hand. Then he jumped to his feet and climbed quickly back up to the flying bridge.

"Our antenna cable has been cut," he said nastily. "Who do you suppose did that, the good fairy? Or that punk on the fuel wharf at Panama City?"

"Why would anyone want to cut your antenna cable?" Laura asked, but even as the words came out of her mouth, she knew the answer. If an antenna cable is cut, there is no way to call for help on the radio.

CHAPTER

6

The *Barbara-Ann* had been moving steadily toward the boat that had launched the distress flare. No more than a thousand yards separated them. Hubbard disengaged the automatic pilot and turned the wheel slightly to the right, turning the *Barbara-Ann* very slightly to the south. He nudged the throttles forward. The sound of the diesels changed pitch.

"What are you doing?" Laura asked.

"I'm going to try to run around them," he said.

"But how do you know they're . . ." She was unable to say the word "pirates." "What you think they are? How do you know they don't need help?"

He looked at her, and she didn't like at all what she saw in his gray eyes. They were cold and scornful.

"If I were you, I'd go below," he said.

"Go to hell!"

He didn't reply. He nudged the throttles again. They were no longer, she saw, headed directly toward the other boat but to the right of it, and the angle was increasing by the moment. The distance between them, however, was closing.

Hubbard, with one hand on the wheel, turned and looked at the other boat through the binoculars. When he took them from his eyes and faced forward, Laura picked them from his hand, leaned against the railing, and looked through them at the other boat. She was frustrated by her ineptitude at finding the other boat and focusing the binoculars. But eventually she could see the other boat.

The men she had seen were no longer waving. She saw one of them hurrying from the forward deck back toward the cockpit. There were two men on the other boat's flying bridge. Then the other boat began to move. A small white bow wave appeared and grew, and then water boiled up behind her.

"They're moving," Laura said to Hubbard.

"I'll bet they are," Hubbard said, turning and snatching the glasses from her.

"Now we're going to have to run," he said. "If they decide to take a shot at us, you're going to make a splendid target up here."

He hung the binoculars around his neck and then went to the hatch in the deck, opened it, and slid down the ladder into the cabin. Laura hesitated a moment and then followed him. She got into the cabin in time to see Hubbard push the twin-engine throttles as far forward as they would go. The dull roar of the diesels changed. The *Barbara-Ann* trembled under the additional power and then seemed to sit back on her haunches.

Things began to slide off shelves and smash together in the refrigerator and cabinets. Two coffee mugs slid off the table, smashed on the deck, and were immediately followed by two plates, knives and forks, and bottles of condiments.

"Damn it," Hubbard said.

"You don't really think you can run away from them in this?" Laura asked.

There was no longer any question in her mind that there was a very good basis for Hubbard's concern and behavior. But she was not surprised. This seemed to be one of those times when nothing that happened could surprise her.

A week ago, she had been a typical unhappy housewife whose husband had turned sour on her. Now he was dead, and she was a hundred miles offshore in the Gulf of Mexico with a man who had been in prison. And they were being pursued by a boatload of men who, if Hubbard was to be believed, wanted to take over the boat and probably throw them into the water.

"I don't know," Hubbard said.

"You don't know what?"

"Whether or not they can catch us," he said. Laura had forgotten that she had asked the question aloud.

"Can they?" She had a sudden thought that what they were doing now was living one of those nightmares in which you were running from something horrible and your legs seemed to be mired in molasses.

"We've got bigger engines than they think we have," he said. "The question is, Are they big enough?"

Both boats, moving south, were traveling on a nearly parallel course, with the other boat three hundred yards off the *Barbara-Ann*'s port and perhaps two hundred yards behind her. As the *Barbara-Ann* continued to run, Laura saw that the distance between them was slowly and steadily closing.

Then, when no more than three hundred yards separated them, there came a whizzing, whistling noise. The same noise came three or four times again, with one whistling whizzing sound immediately after another. The mirror mounted on the cabin bulkhead cracked, and large pieces fell away and crashed onto the deck of the cabin.

"Oh, shit," Hubbard said bitterly.

She looked at him and realized that he was not unhappy because the pounding of the *Barbara-Ann* through the water had cracked the mirror. The incredible truth seemed to be that they were being shot at. There were four small holes in the windows in the rear of the cabin.

"I've had enough of this crap," Hubbard said suddenly and angrily. "Come here."

She went to him, and he took her hands and put them on the throttles.

"When I give you the word," he said, "you pull back on the throttles. And keep your hands on them. When I give you the word again, shove them as far forward as they'll go."

"What are you going to do?" she asked.

"For Christ's sake, Mrs. Wood, just do what I tell you."

He went aft in the cabin and picked up the Army rifle. Then he went, ducking, out onto the rear deck, and lay down. There was a hatch built into the railing so that a heavy fish could be brought aboard easily. He pulled it open toward him and then put the rifle to his shoulder.

She realized numbly that he was going to shoot at the other boat.

There came more whistling, whizzing noises. There was the sound of shattering glass, and then something slapped her hard on the breast. She looked down at herself first in surprise and then in horror. There was a rip in her blouse, and then the material turned red with blood.

She'd been shot.

She screamed loudly enough to make him turn from the rifle and look over his shoulder at her. She pulled the blouse away from her body and saw that the blood was coming through her brassiere. She looked at Hubbard desperately, seeking help. She felt faint.

"Chop the power," he shouted.

She stared at him without comprehension. Hadn't he seen what had happened to her?

"Chop the fucking power," he shouted.

There was a tone in his voice that frightened her to the point where she was more afraid of not doing what he was ordering her to do than anything else.

She turned to the controls and pulled back on the throttles. Instantly, the *Barbara-Ann* began to slow as if she were being held back by some kind of force. The bow seemed to bury itself in the water ahead.

Laura looked down at her bosom again. There was a large red patch on her blouse. When, without thinking about it, she moved her hand toward her breast, several drops of blood fell onto her hand. She stared at them in horror and disbelief and then turned to look at Hubbard.

He was on his stomach, with the rifle to his shoulder, aiming in through the fish port in the railing. He would shoot now, she thought, and she braced herself for the noise the rifle would make. She looked down again at the bright red drops of blood on her hand.

Was she going to die out here in the Gulf? Was that how this nightmare was going to end? She thought of Little Art. What was going to happen to him?

There was no sound of rifle fire from the rear deck. She looked back at Hubbard impatiently. He was doing exactly what he had been doing the last time she looked at him, lying on his stomach and aiming the rifle through the fish port.

The *Barbara-Ann* slowed even more so that it was hardly moving. Its motion changed from an up-and-down movement from bow to stern to a side-to-side rolling in the swells. Still Hubbard did nothing.

"Shoot!" she heard herself cry, half angry, half begging.

The rifle barked twice. The sound, although she had expected it, was sharper and louder than she had imagined it would be. It made her ears ring. She saw something shiny flying through the air and realized that it was a fired cartridge. Then Hubbard fired twice again and then two times more. A steady stream of shiny cartridge cases flew through the air. She heard the tinkling sound they made as they struck the walls of the cabin and fell onto the deck.

Then he began to fire steadily, for she could no longer count the shots.

Then he laid the rifle down on the deck and started for the cabin on his hands and knees.

"Go," he shouted.

Laura turned and put her hands to the throttles and pushed them forward. She heard one of the diesel engines growl and then roar. She saw what had happened: The blood had made her hand slip off the left throttle lever. The *Barbara-Ann* yawed for a moment until she pushed the throttle forward with her other hand; then the other diesel engine surged to full power.

Hubbard was now on his feet and in the cabin.

"Jesus," he said, looking at her chest. "Those bastards!"

"I guess I'm shot," she said inanely. She put her hand to her breast.

Hubbard pushed her hand out of the way. He put both hands to the opening of her blouse and ripped it open. She saw that the left cup of her brassiere was blood-soaked. Blood was actually dripping from it. Hubbard put both hands to her brassiere and gave a yank, ripping it down the front.

She saw the wound. Blood ran out of it. Hubbard reached into his pocket and took out a handkerchief and laid it over the wound.

"Press that as hard as you can," he ordered.

She put her fingers on the handkerchief and pressed it against her breast so hard that it hurt.

Hubbard went to the controls, synchronized the engines, and spun the wheel to correct their course. Then he looked over his shoulder at the boat behind them. Laura followed his glance. The boat was now sidewards to them, still moving fast but obviously turning away from them.

"Did you kill them?" she asked.

"Christ, I hope not," he said. "The last thing I need is some macho Latino swearing revenge on his sainted mother's grave."

"But they're not chasing us anymore," she said.

"I let them know," he said, "that if it came down to it, I would kill a couple of them."

He looked over at the compass, made another course correction, and reengaged the automatic pilot. Then he turned to her. "I'd better have a look at that," he said. "Are you about to faint on me?"

"I feel a little woozy," Laura said.

"Damn," he said impatiently. "See if you can make it to the couch. Put your head between your legs."

She walked across the cabin, carefully avoiding the broken coffee mugs and the shards of mirror glass, and sat down on the couch. She did not feel faint and did not put her head between her legs.

"Put your head between your legs," Hubbard ordered from across the cabin.

She glared at him and saw that he was wrestling with the snap catches of a first aid kit mounted on the bulkhead. She told herself that she had just been shot and that people who were shot fainted. She lowered her head between her legs.

In a moment he was beside her on his knees, putting the first aid kit on the cushion of the couch beside her.

"That ought to do it," he said. "Sit up."

She sat up. She was suddenly aware that for all practical purposes, she was naked above the waist.

He leaned toward her and gently pushed her hand away from the handkerchief. Then he removed the handkerchief. She looked down and saw the wound and the blood running from it.

He tore open an envelope from the first aid kit and mopped at the blood with the bandage it contained. He looked intently at the wound and then pinched it painfully between his fingers.

Then he laughed, pleased. "Relax," he said. "You haven't been shot."

Laura was furious. "What do you mean I haven't been shot?"

"You were hit by a piece of flying glass," he explained as he looked into the first aid kit again. "Probably from the bottle of bourbon those bastards blew away."

"That isn't being shot?" she asked icily.

"If you'd been shot," he said condescendingly, "you'd know it."

He tore open another envelope and mopped more blood away, and then he took an aerosol can of antiseptic and sprayed the wounded area generously. The antiseptic was cold, and it stung. And, she was infuriated to see, it made her nipple grow erect.

He mopped at the area again—as if he were mopping a floor, she thought—and then he opened another, smaller envelope and took a smaller bandage from it. He laid that across the wound.

"Hold it," he ordered, and she put her fingers on it. He took out a roll of adhesive tape and ripped off two pieces from it. Then he matter-of-factly taped the small bandage in place.

"That'll do it," he said.

"How do you know there's not a bullet in there?" she asked.

He smiled at her, that infuriating superior smile.

"God is great," he said, cheerfully solemn. "And God is good. He wouldn't dream of ruining a splendid matched pair like that."

"You son of a bitch," Laura snapped.

"Now, that's no way to talk to a man who has just bandaged your boob," he said, and got up. He grew serious. "I'll have a look at it later."

Laura thought but didn't say: The hell you will, you male chauvinist bastard!

"Why don't you go wash yourself off," he suggested

reasonably. "And then clean this mess up."

He snapped the first aid kit closed and then put it back in the wall mount he'd taken it from. He picked up the binoculars and walked toward the aft deck. She saw his eyes move to her breasts. She was simultaneously furious with him for the unabashed look and with herself for sitting there with everything hanging out.

She got up and went to the cabin. She undressed and washed herself. Blood was even on her legs, where it had dripped down onto her lap. She washed herself thoroughly and then started to put on a clean brassiere. She almost immediately found that it wasn't going to work. The upward lift of the cup pressed painfully against the bandage. She would have to go without a bra, and that meant putting her nipples on display for him to look at. Damn him!

She went back into her suitcase and found a terry-cloth blouse that was thick enough, she hoped, to preserve her modesty.

Then she thought that she was being ridiculous. He had already seen her breasts. And he had, she thought next, quite literally just saved her life. Finally, she thought: The only reason there was no bullet in there, or for that matter in my head, was pure luck. And then she realized that that wasn't true, either. The reason there was no bullet in her, the reason she was alive, was that he had driven the other boat off with his rifle fire. I actually owe someone my life, she thought.

And he knew it, the patronizing male bastard!

She put on a clean pair of slacks and went back into the cabin. He was at the controls, with the rifle on the shelf in front of them. He was loading cartridges into the magazine.

"That thieving son of a bitch Crawford's been into the ammunition," he said.

"I beg your pardon?"

"Crawford," he said. "The bastard poaches deer, and he just helped himself to my ammunition."

The implication, she realized, was that he expected to have to use the rifle again. She felt a sudden chill.

"Are they going to come after us again?"

"I don't think they will," he said. "But most of those bastards have friends. Apparently all they had was Uzis. That's why they broke off."

"Uzis? What's that?"

He turned around, picked something off the counter, and tossed it to her. She caught it with a reflex action. It was a fired bullet, she realized, a small piece of battered lead and copper that had made the whistling, whizzing noise. It had been intended to kill her.

"The Israelis make a fine 9-mm submachine gun," he said. "A guy named Uzi invented it. That's what they were shooting at us. It doesn't have the range of the 7.62-mm I was using, so they backed off. Uzi's cost fifteen hundred, two thousand dollars. Doesn't bother those drug guys. They've got more money than God."

He finished loading the magazine in his hand, installed it in the rifle, and then went to the rear of the cabin, where there was a rack concealed by the curtain over the windows.

"You want to start cleaning up?" he asked, making it an order. "That broken glass is dangerous."

She flared. "What are you going to be doing while I'm cleaning?"

"I thought I'd see if I can't fix the antenna cable," he said. "It would be nice to be able to call for help if something else happens."

As she was cleaning up the cabin, he came into it and went to the controls and slowed the engines.

"What are you slowing down for?" she demanded.

"Because as fast as we were going takes a lot more fuel than we have," he said. "Anyway, I think we're far enough away from them to be safe."

"Oh," she said, a little sorry that she had challenged him.

"The antenna cable is beyond fixing," he said. "At least out here."

"Oh."

"Does your . . . are you in pain?" he asked.

"Not much," she said bravely. The truth was that it stung just a little, and she was furious with herself for playing for his sympathy.

"Bourbon's as good as anything for pain, I think," he said, and then left the cabin and went to the flying bridge. He gets to drive, she thought, while I'm on my hands and knees cleaning up the mess.

That was really a cheap crack of his, she thought angrily: "God wouldn't think of ruining a fine matched set like that." He had no right to say something like that. It was the sort of thing you could expect from someone who had been thrown out of the Navy and now lived with the madam of a whorehouse.

But the anger didn't last. It soon was replaced by her thought that his crack had been a compliment, or as close to a compliment as Jack Hubbard probably would ever come.

When she had finished cleaning up the mess in the cabin, she went to the galley and made him a hoagie, slicing a length of stale French bread, covering the bottom with an array of cold cuts and cheese and tomatoes and onions, and then sprinkling it liberally with Italian dressing. She took a bottle of beer from the refrigerator, stuck it in the waistband of her pants, and then climbed the interior ladder to the deck to give it to him.

She looked around. There was nothing on the horizon in any direction.

"They're gone," he said.

She handed him the sandwich. When she pulled the beer from her waistband, he chuckled.

Then she went down and made herself a sandwich and carried it and another bottle of beer up to deck.

"Why did they want your boat?" she asked.

"I hope that all it was was they wanted it to carry grass," he said. When her eyebrows raised quizzically, he said, "You'd be surprised how much grass a boat this size will carry. They'd take maybe two, three tons in fifty-pound bales off a mother ship, run this boat into a cove or up a river, and unload it. There's places to do that from one tip of Florida to the other."

"What would they do with the boat?"

"Oh, if they had a really plush yacht; they might take it to Panama or some place and sell it. A boat like this they'd just take back out in the deep water, shoot some holes in the hull, and let it sink."

"And they'd have killed us to get it? I mean, I know they would. But it still seems unreal."

"You bet your ass they would have. Those drug guys scare hell out of me."

"You didn't seem afraid," she said without thinking.

"You weren't looking close, lady," he said. He changed the subject. "This is . . . was . . . a good sandwich."

"You want another one?" she asked, pleased at the compliment.

"Later," he said. "It was also a large sandwich."

"Say when," she said.

"OK."

Laura picked up one of the deck chairs that had fallen over when he had been running the *Barbara-Ann* fast and set it up so that she could sit looking aft. They rode in a silence broken only by the dull roar of the diesels for ten minutes.

"What happened with you in the Navy?" Laura finally asked.

"What?"

"What happened, what kind of trouble were you in in the Navy?"

"What makes you think I was in trouble in the Navy?"

"The old chief told me he heard that," Laura said.

"The old chief, like most old chiefs, doesn't know what he's talking about," Hubbard insisted. "Not that it matters, but when I resigned from the Navy, I was a chief warrant officer."

"Why did you resign?"

"Barbara-Ann wanted me to spend more time at home," he said.

"Your wife?"

"Right."

"Who you named the boat after?"

"Right."

"Where is she now?" Laura asked. Maybe he was a widower, she thought suddenly.

"If there's any justice at all," Hubbard said, "she's dying slowly and painfully of terminal social disease."

"I guess you're divorced?" she asked.

"Listen," he said, suddenly very angry. "Just because you caught me looking at your boobs doesn't mean you're entitled to my life's story. That comes under the category, Mrs. Wood, of none of your fucking business."

He was so angry that she was frightened. She wanted to flee below, but she forced herself to stay. Four or five minutes later, he said very softly: "I bought this boat at auction. The guy who owned it first had cancer or something, and he wanted his family to get double indemnity on his insurance, so he took it out and tried to have an accident. He set it on fire and then sat down on the couch and blew his brains out with a revolver.

She looked at him in surprise. "The poor man," she said.

He ignored her reply and went on: "He didn't know what he was doing, so what the Coast Guard found was a charred body and a burned-out hull. When I bought it, it didn't even look bad from the outside. But inside it was really rotten and smelled worse, and with burned-out engines, of course, it was as useless as teats on a boar hog. That's why I named her the *Barbara-Ann*."

Laura had never heard such bitterness in a human voice before.

"My God, what did she do to you?" she asked, turning to look at him.

Hubbard turned away from the controls and went down the ladder to the cockpit without saying another word.

CHAPTER
7

There was a strange feeling later that day and into the night of being the only people on earth. Or at least on the Gulf of Mexico. The weather remained good, and the seas were long and gentle rolling swells through which the *Barbara-Ann* moved steadily with a pleasant rolling motion.

Sea gulls appeared from somewhere when Laura threw the debris from the shot-up cabin and the garbage over the stern. She opened the windows in the forward bulkhead of the cabin to get rid of the smell and the fumes from the shattered half-gallon bottle of bourbon. She found a vacuum cleaner in one of the cabinets, and when she had finished using it to clean the cabin, she was aware of a feeling of satisfaction that she sometimes felt after cleaning her house.

If it were not for the bullet holes in the windows and the bandage on her breast, it would have been easy to dismiss what had happened to them as something she had seen in a television movie.

Hubbard seemed to be avoiding her. When she went into the cabin after his outburst, he went back onto the deck. And when she finished cleaning the cabin and went on the deck herself, he was back in the cabin.

She had been alone on the deck when the sun set. The sun seemed larger than she ever remembered it, and it was beautiful as it sank below the horizon.

She went below shortly afterward, for the temperature had quickly dropped with the sun gone. This time, he did not go back onto the deck.

Laura asked him if he was hungry. He shook his head and said, "I'm starved."

She prepared a full meal, and they ate together at the table in the cabin. Afterward, he showed her how the LORAN III, the long-range navigation system, worked and marked their position on the plastic covering a chart of the west coast of Florida and the Gulf of Mexico. They were then about one hundred fifty miles south of Panama City and as far west of Saint Petersburg.

Hubbard showed her how the radar worked and told her that he had it set on its greatest range, about twenty-five miles.

"I'm going to try to get some sleep," he said. "If a blip gets within five miles, wake me up." He pointed out the five-mile ring on the radar screen. "In any event, wake me at midnight if I'm not up."

He went into the cabin and then reappeared in a moment to show her how to work the broadcast radio receiver in case she couldn't get the television to work. Then he disappeared again.

She heard the sound of an electric motor and then him singing. Then she put the two together. The electric motor was operating a water pump, and he was taking a shower. A mental image of Hubbard in the shower popped into her mind, and she forced it out by trying to capture a picture on the television screen by manipulating the antenna.

He did not wake at midnight, and for a couple of

minutes she decided to let him sleep. Finally, she decided that she had better wake him up. She went to the cabin door and pushed it open. Her face flushed. Hubbard was sleeping naked, on his back, his arms at his sides, his legs spread. He had a full-grown erection.

She quickly pulled the door closed. Her academic knowledge, from some book she'd read, that the male animal routinely has a dozen or more erections in his sleep and that what she had inadvertently happened to see was perfectly natural and innocent did not permit her to erase the image of his erection from her mind.

She knocked loudly on the door and called his name. When he came into the cabin a minute later, fully dressed, she could still see it.

"Is there any coffee left?" he asked.

"I'll make some," she said. Her voice sounded strange to her, but he didn't seem to notice.

By the time he had finished using the LORAN III to compute their new position and had done other mysterious things to the controls and navigation equipment, the coffee was done. When she handed him the cup and their fingers touched, she felt a stirring in her middle.

Furious with herself, she announced that she was going to go to bed.

"I wouldn't take a shower with that bandage on," he said, "if you can do without one. If you really need one, try to keep it dry."

"I can wait," she said, wondering why she was embarrassed.

"We'll get you to a doctor at Port Boca Grande," he said.

"Do I need a doctor?" she asked. She hadn't thought about that.

"There may be a piece of glass in there," he told her. "And you should get a tetanus shot."

"What are we going to do at Port Boca Grande?" she asked.

"I'm good, Mrs. Wood," he said, "but I'm no miracle man. I can't work alone, legend to the contrary."

"If we're going to be that close to Fort Myers," she said, "I'd like to check on my little boy."

She could tell from the look on his face that he hadn't considered that and didn't like it now that she had brought it up.

"We can get you a car at Port Boca Grande," he said. "But the less time we lose, the better."

"I understand," she said. She walked to the cabin door. "Good night," she said.

He looked at her as if surprised. "Good night, Mrs. Wood," he said.

'She closed the door behind her, slid the locking latch home, and carefully pulled the terrycloth shirt over her head. She went to the mirror, turned the light on, and examined her breast. The black and blue of a bruise showed from under the bandage.

She took her slacks off and lay down on the bed. The sheets were still warm from Hubbard's body, and there was the scent of him. The mental image of him on his back, with the full erection, came back into her mind.

She was, she realized, with mingled annoyance and chagrin, sexually excited. There was an explanation for it, Laura told herself. For one thing, it had been a long time since she had been with a man. She hadn't been with that many men before she married Art. But at the beginning with Art, there had been a good deal of plain and fancy sex. That had lasted until she had become pregnant, or more specifically, until her pregnancy had become obvious.

Then there had been sex less and less often. And after Little Art was born, it had never been the same. Not that she didn't feel the same. Art was the one who had changed, or at least as far as she was concerned. He had had women, but only rarely had one of the women been she.

For the last eight months or so, it had never been she, not since the night he had taken it out on her, called her those obscene names, punched her with such fury in the stomach because he couldn't get it up and she couldn't get it up for him. After that he hadn't come near her, and she had been relieved.

So she was, as it said in the women's magazines, "sexually unfulfilled," which meant horny. Then Hubbard had done the macho thing, the warrior protecting the helpless princess. Then he'd lain there with his thing sticking up like the Leaning Tower of Pisa. It was perfectly understandable why she was horny. It was understandable, but it didn't make things any better.

She tossed around on a bed redolent with male smell. There was only one thing to do about it, she decided. She certainly couldn't get involved sexually with a man like Hubbard. She could think about it, but it had to stop right there. She permitted the mental image of Hubbard on his back to come back into her mind, and then she slipped her hand into her pants.

The *Barbara-Ann* made landfall at half past seven the next morning. Laura knew from looking at the chart and from the strength of the television picture that they were south of Sarasota. As the land mass gradually came into focus, she recognized exactly where they were, just north of the north end of Gasparilla Island. Hubbard had drawn a dotted line on the chart, showing where he wanted to go. He had hit it, she realized, almost on the nose.

Hubbard took the *Barbara-Ann* under the highway bridge into Charlotte Harbor and twenty minutes later turned out of the main channel into the channel leading to Port Boca Grande.

"Who are we going to see here?" Laura asked hesitantly.

"Somebody who may or may not figure he owes your husband something," he replied. Then he added: "You want to go forward and handle the line?"

Laura wondered what kind of a man here could possibly owe Art something. Port Boca Grande had at one time been the base for Portuguese sponge fishermen, a business that had nearly been killed by the invention of plastic sponges. Although there was now a small rebirth of that trade, based on the superiority of Mother Nature's product over the chemist's, Port Boca Grande was now nothing more than a small, nearly deserted port at the end of a narrow two-lane road. By water, Fort Myers was twenty-five miles down Pine Island Sound and then twenty miles up the Caloosahatchee River. By road, Laura knew that to get home she would have to drive all the way up one side of Charlotte Harbor, cross a bridge there, and then drive another thirty miles to Fort Myers.

Unintentionally, Hubbard was sure, Laura faced aft as she knelt on the deck to take the line from its hatch. The terrycloth shirt she was wearing fell away from her body, and he could see her unrestrained breasts beneath it.

Jesus Christ, she has a set of knockers!

If you have seen two, boy, you've seen them all.

Mother Nature, you're a bitch, all right. Give you half a chance, and you'll have a man making an ass of himself over a set of glands.

Laura glanced up at the bridge and caught him looking. Instinctively, she put her hand to her shirt and then turned her body away from him.

They're all the same, she thought. Only one thing on their minds. I wonder if he thinks I did that on purpose. I'm not that kind of woman. Or am I? Did I subconsciously bend over that way so he could see down my shirt?

They were approaching the pilings of a fuel wharf now. A large, full-bearded man in a T-shirt stretched taut by his massive chest and upper arms was standing on the wharf, supporting himself with both elbows on the top of a piling. As the *Barbara-Ann*'s bow approached, he stood erect and smiled. He reached out and took the line from Laura's hand as Hubbard put the boat in reverse and she stopped.

Laura moved quickly aft and handed the bearded man the aft line. He quickly made it fast and then did something astonishing. Smiling broadly, showing a lot of white natural teeth and a handful of gold teeth, he came to attention, saluted crisply, and bellowed, "Permission to come aboard, sir!"

Hubbard came down the ladder from the flying bridge, sliding down the stainless-steel handrails, not using the steps. There was a warm, gentle smile on his face. Laura had never seen him look that way before.

"Pombal," he said. "How the hell are you?"

Hubbard jumped up on the wharf and put out his hand. The large man ignored it and wrapped his massive arms around Hubbard's back and lifted him off his feet.

"How the hell goes it, Skipper?" he asked. "Mother of God, it's good to see you!"

"You, too, you fat son of a bitch," Hubbard said when Pombal finally set him back on his feet.

"I'm not fat, I'm well fed," Pombal said. He looked at Laura. "Nice," he said. "Very nice."

"Mrs. Wood," Hubbard said. "This is Tony Pombal."

"Pleased to meet you," Pombal said. Then he stared at Hubbard with a puzzled look on his face. "Wood?" he asked.

Hubbard nodded his head.

Pombal's eyes took another, closer, less friendly look at Laura and then moved from her to the *Barbara-Ann*. With a grace that, considering his size, was astonishing, he jumped onto the rear deck and scooped something up from the floor before repeating the quick bending motion twice more. Then, holding three fired cartridges in his open palm, he looked up at Hubbard.

"What the hell have you been up to, Skipper?" he asked.

"Take a look at the windows," Hubbard said.

Pombal did as he was told; he walked to the holes in the windows and examined them carefully.

"Somebody tried to take the boat, Tony," Hubbard said. "Maybe ninety miles out of Panama City."

"And you took them out, right? Serves the bastards right. I hope you fed the bodies to the crabs," Pombal said coldly.

"I changed their minds about how easy it looked," Hubbard said.

"You didn't blow them away?" Pombal asked. Laura saw that he was both surprised and disappointed.

"I put a couple of rounds through their radar," Hubbard said. "And they're going to have to replace the windshield."

"Was that before or after they tried to blow you away?" Pombal asked. "What was that, 9 mm?"

"Yeah," Hubbard said. "I found a bullet in the cabin. Uzis, I think."

"Plural?"

"Yeah," Hubbard said. "Plural."

"You should have blown them away, Skipper. It's even legal. What did the Coast Guard have to say?"

"The Coast Guard doesn't know."

"What you should have done is blow them away and then called the Coast Guard," Pombal said.

"For one thing," Hubbard replied, "they have too many friends. I didn't want to declare war on the Colombian Volunteer Navy."

"You're getting soft in your old age," Pombal said. "The way you handle people like that is feed them to the crabs."

It was not, Laura realized, a philosophic discussion. The bearded man was deadly serious in his belief that Hubbard should have killed the people on the boat. She sensed that both he and Hubbard had killed people before and had not been very deeply upset by it.

"You said," Pombal said, "for one thing. What's the other thing?"

"You still got a soldering iron?" Hubbard replied. "Vermin got into my antenna feed." He pointed to the side of the cabin.

Tony Pombal took a quick look and then peered up at Hubbard.

"It took a big set of dikes to cut that cable," he said. "Where did that happen?"

"It had to be in Panama City," Hubbard said. "When I took on fuel."

"You want a new lead," Pombal said. "You don't want to splice that."

"You got one?"

"Sure I got one," Pombal said. "But first we go get some breakfast." He jumped nimbly onto the wharf and then turned and offered his hand to Laura. "You, too, honey," he said. He jerked her effortlessly onto the wharf.

"You have fuel, Tony?" Hubbard asked.

"You didn't come here to top off your tanks," Tony Pombal said. "What the hell's going on, anyway?"

"I'll tell you as soon as you give me a cup of coffee," Hubbard said.

"In other words," Pombal replied, "not in front of her, huh?"

"Arthur Wood dumped his Cessna while landing off Fort Jefferson in the Dry Tortugas," Hubbard said.

"So I heard. To tell you the truth, I didn't cry a whole hell of a lot when I heard about it," Pombal said. He looked at Laura again and very carefully asked, "What's that got to do with you and me?"

"I owed him," Hubbard said.

"Shit!" Pombal said, and then cleared his throat and spat.

"I figure I did, Tony."

"And this is the bereaved widow, right? And she laid that you owed him bullshit on you, right?" Pombal said disgustedly, nodding his glowering head at Laura.

"She doesn't get the insurance unless she can recover

the body,'' Hubbard began.

"She can recover the body?'' Pombal interrupted. "Shit. Unless you recover the body for her. Right?''

"I'll pay you whatever you figure is right,'' Hubbard said.

"Shit again. If you figure you owe him, that means I owe him, too. And where the fuck is Crawford? If I owe that bastard, then that skinny old fart owes him, too. Just as much as anybody.''

"He had a chance to make a couple of thousand dollars,'' Hubbard said. "He said he'd come if I really needed him.''

"In a pig's ass he will,'' Pombal said. "Crawford takes care of number one and number one only.''

"OK,'' Hubbard said. "I'm not going to argue with you much less plead with you. Just fix the fucking antenna and I'll shove off.''

"In a pig's ass you will,'' Pombal said. "You know I couldn't let you do that. I don't like it one fucking bit, Skipper, but I'm in. You knew goddamn well what I'd do, too, you bastard.''

"I need you, Tony,'' Hubbard said. "I'll make it up to you.''

"Yeah, bullshit,'' Pombal said. "Well, come on. The old lady's waiting.'' He waved his hand down the wharf, where a battered vehicle with "POMBAL FISHERIES'' painted on the door waited.

CHAPTER

8

Mr. and Mrs. Antonio Pombal lived in a sprawling frame house mounted on pilings in the sand of Gasparilla Island. Mrs. Evangeline "Angy" Pombal, who answered the door with a small child on one hip and another clinging to her skirts, was a chubby woman with a bright smile. It was easy to see beneath the layer of smooth fat on her face and arms the beautiful girl she once had been. She kissed Hubbard warmly on the cheek and then offered her hand to Laura.

"I hope you like fish for breakfast," she said. "These two do."

"Love it," Laura said. She could never remember having been offered fish for breakfast.

Tony Pombal broke out a bottle of bourbon and poured three inches of it into two glasses.

"Up the bastards' asses, Skipper," he said, raising his glass to Hubbard.

"With an eight-foot oar," Hubbard replied, and they sipped almost formally, ritually, at their straight whiskey.

It was not, Laura sensed, a chance exchange of masculine obscenities. It had some meaning, made some reference to other times and other places. It had something to do with Pombal calling Hubbard Skipper.

Laura went into the kitchen after Mrs. Pombal, getting there in time to see her take an oblong pan from an enormous refrigerator. The pan was full of large fish filets, floating in butter and topped with slices of lemon and dusted with paprika.

"All ready for the oven," Mrs. Pombal said. "Tony said Jack would be in here first thing in the morning. I guess he read his mind. It won't take but a minute."

"I guess Tony and Jack are pretty close," Laura said, more than a little ashamed that she was snooping for information.

"Huh," Mrs. Pombal snorted. After she had slid the pan with the fish into the broiler section of the oven, she took Laura's arm and led her out of the kitchen into a room dominated by a four-foot-long statue of Christ on the cross, and an eighteen by twenty-four inch framed lithograph of the bleeding heart of Jesus. Laura saw that one corner held a huge television set, on the top of which were a dozen or more video cassettes. There were framed photographs on the wall, to which Mrs. Pombal pointed. The first showed nine sailors in blue uniforms. They were gathered around Jack Hubbard, the only officer. Laura spotted Tony Pombal, beardless and fifty pounds lighter, and Chet Crawford, looking as he had looked when she had seen him in New Orleans.

"That was the original SEAL team," Mrs. Pombal said, "when they formed. And this was taken in Nam." She pointed to a photograph showing the same men sprawled on a beach somewhere in the bright sunlight. None of them was wearing more clothes than a pair of cut-off pants; they were all armed to the teeth, and there were whiskey bottles and beer cans all over.

There were only three men in the third picture: Hubbard, Pombal, and Crawford. It was a nightclub photograph. They were all in civilian clothes.

"God let these three come home," Mrs. Pombal said softly, making the sign of the cross on her ample bosom.

"I don't know what a SEAL team is," Laura said.

"That figures," Hubbard said coldly from the door. "What are you doing nosing around in here?"

"Shut your nasty mouth, Jack," Mrs. Pombal said. "I showed her. What's wrong with that? You're afraid they'll find out you're human?" Mrs. Pombal asked, and added sarcastically, "Mr. Tough Guy."

Hubbard walked into the kitchen without replying.

"Don't pay any attention to him," Mrs. Pombal said. "You have to understand him."

"The way to understand Jack Hubbard, Mrs. Wood," Tony Pombal said flatly, "is to remember that his bite is worse than his bark."

"The fish is probably ready," his wife said to him. "Go in and eat."

The meal was huge. The broiled filets and a mound of home-fried potatoes and sliced tomatoes were spiced in a way Laura had never tasted before. Laura was surprised to see that she had eaten everything Mrs. Pombal had heaped on her plate.

Then the plates were taken away, and a cake and a coffeepot were set on the table.

"He went down in that 182 of his?" Pombal asked, getting down to business.

"Who went down in a 182?" Mrs. Pombal asked. "Oh, you mean that pool hall sharpie who was out here to see you?"

Laura sensed that "pool hall sharpie" was about the worst thing Angy Pombal could bring herself to say about anyone.

"What did he want with you?" Hubbard asked.

"What do you think?" Pombal replied, looking a little uneasy.

"Did he spell it out?" Hubbard pursued.

"I didn't give him the chance, Jack."

"I wish you had," Hubbard replied.

"The only way to do with those people," Angy Pombal pontificated, "is to stay two miles away from them. Three miles."

"Angy," Pombal said. "Close your fat mouth. This is Mrs. Wood."

Angy Pombal pursed her lips, and her eyebrows went up, but she did not apologize.

She's looking at me as if she can't understand how I can hide the scarlet A on my forehead, Laura thought uncomfortably. And then she had an irreverent thought: If she could see the bandage on my breast, she'd think that's where they branded the A with a red-hot iron.

"What I meant before," Hubbard said, "was that if he had made you some kind of a proposition, we'd know for sure that he was in that business."

"Ah, come on, Jack," Pombal said. "You know how long he's been in the business."

"That was there," Hubbard said. "This is here. And Mrs. Wood says she doesn't think so."

"What do you expect her to say?"

"She says there was no money," Hubbard went on. "And he was not the guy who could squirrel money away."

"What the hell difference does it make, anyway," Pombal asked, "one way or the other? If he was carrying something and somebody knew he was, they'll be out there looking. If he wasn't, they won't be."

"How soon could somebody get out there?" Hubbard asked.

"Ordinarily, within thirty-six hours. I mean with the barge and the whole business. But there's been six- to eight-foot seas. I couldn't get out there myself until yesterday . . ."

"You were out there yesterday?" Hubbard interrupted him. "What for?"

"I think maybe I found me a ship," he said, looking uncomfortable.

"My husband, the treasure hunter," Angy said. "One of these days he's going to find one, and then we eat off solid gold plates."

"How close were you to Fort Jefferson?"

"Is that where he dumped it?" Pombal asked, and then answered the question: "Not far."

"And there was nobody there?"

"Nobody," Pombal said. "But that was yesterday."

"I want to get out there today," Hubbard said. "I need a car, Tony."

"You got one," Tony said. "You can have Angy's. What for?"

"Mrs. Wood has to see a doctor," Hubbard said. "She cut herself on a piece of flying glass. And she wants to see her kid."

"She has to go to Fort Myers, you mean?" Tony asked. "You're welcome to the car, Jack, but you'd do better to go by boat. There's a hell of a detour."

Hubbard nodded and then asked, "What was the water like?"

"Clear," Pombal replied. "If you can find it, you can probably see it from the surface."

"Yeah, and by the time I get there, you won't be able to see five feet," Hubbard said.

"I've got the magnetometer on the boat," Pombal said.

"Can you take off now?"

"I can leave here about five this afternoon," Pombal answered reluctantly.

"How long will it take you to get there?"

"I make seven knots if the wind is right," Pombal said. "I'm not engined the way you are."

"Then twenty, twenty-one hours?"

"Something like that."

"If we don't get delayed in Fort Myers," Hubbard said. "I can be out there by midnight or one o'clock."

Laura knew that the remark was directed at her. "How long is it going to take you to replace my antenna cable?"

"It better be done by now," Tony said. "I told them, and I told them to top off your tanks."

"Good man," Hubbard said. Laura saw how Tony basked in Hubbard's approval.

"I'll also bring some food," Tony said. "Angy can shop while I'm getting ready."

"Who are you going to bring with you?"

"Angy's brother Sidonio," Pombal said. "He's a good man."

"Tell him what he's getting into," Hubbard said.

"He owes me," Pombal said simply.

"Ask around," Hubbard said. "If you can."

"About what?"

"What was Wood doing out there?"

"What was he supposed to be doing?"

"Picking up passengers from a yacht."

"Maybe he was," Tony said. "I'll find out what I can."

As the *Barbara-Ann* headed toward the marina in Fort Myers, Laura got out of her deck chair and went and stood beside Hubbard.

"What's a SEAL?" she asked.

"An aquatic mammal," Hubbard replied.

"You know what I mean."

"The Navy's answer to the Green Berets," he said. "The Navy can't stand to be one-upped by the Army."

"What does it mean?"

"Sea, air, land," he said. "Very cute."

"What did you do?"

"Mostly, we blew things up," he said. "Things up and people away." He changed the subject again. "How long is it going to take you to see your doctor and get a shot, check on your kid, and get back to the marina?"

"I don't know."

"You understand, Mrs. Wood," he said. "The sooner we get out there, the better."

"I'll hurry."

"Who's taking care of your kid?"

"The woman next door," she told him.

He nodded. She wasn't sure if it meant approval or meant that he expected something like that from her.

"Go tie us up," he ordered.

Hubbard stayed on the flying bridge until Laura had walked into the marina office and shop complex; then he went into the cabin. He put on a set of battered coveralls, opened the engine compartment, and spent thirty minutes checking the engines and the various pumps. Then he went back to the cabin and very carefully cleaned and lubricated the M1A rifle he had fired at the boat off Panama City.

The M1A was a modification of the Army's M14 rifle, which fired the 7.62-mm NATO cartridge. It differed from the M14 only in that it could not be switched to fully automatic. That suited him fine. He'd fired enough fully automatic weapons to know that they wasted a lot of ammunition. He remembered that Chet Crawford had, in the ancient tradition of chief petty officers, borrowed most of the ammunition he'd had aboard for the rifle.

Pombal probably had a supply, but he hadn't wanted to ask him for some in front of Angy. And there was no way he could be sure that Pombal would bring any when he came out to the Dry Tortugas on his work boat.

"Goddamn that wimp," he said aloud about Chet Crawford. He was going to have to go into town and buy ammunition. He simply couldn't go out there with less than sixty rounds for the M1A and a couple of boxes of 00 buckshot for the riot gun.

He took a quick shower and put on a pair of slacks and a sports shirt and a new pair of loafers. Then he went ashore. He checked the Yellow Pages of the Fort

Myers telephone book for sporting goods stores and then took a cab to what looked to be the largest one.

First he asked for two boxes of 12-gauge 00 buckshot shells and then for .308 Winchester 186-grain soft point cartridges. A number of manufacturers made sporting rifles for the cartridge.

"You want to buy them by the hundred," the salesman said. "I can make you a deal on some GI armor-piercing."

"What would I do with armor-piercing bullets?" Hubbard asked innocently.

"What you do is take a file and file the tip of the nose off," the salesman told him. "That turns them into a soft point. Really plays hell with a deer. Just between you and me, the GI cartridges are much more powerful, sort of a magnum, than the standard commercial cartridges."

"No kidding?" Hubbard asked innocently.

"Take my word for it," the salesman said confidently. "You get a better shell for a lot less money."

"You're sure about this?" Hubbard asked suspiciously.

"You got my word on it," the salesman said.

"Well," Hubbard said after a moment's hesitation, "I'll take a chance. I'd better take two hundred. My father-in-law has a .308, too. Jesus, how much did you say they are?"

The salesman told him. Hubbard looked into his wallet and counted his money.

"So does my brother-in-law," Hubbard said. "And if I don't get some for him—Christ . . . are you sure about this? It seems too good to be true."

"You can take it to the bank," the salesman said.

"Three hundred, then," Hubbard said, making up his mind.

The salesman took his money, made change, and handed him the ammunition, still in GI boxes, in a heavy carton that had originally held shot shells. He didn't ask for Hubbard's name much less for any identification.

Hubbard flagged a cab and ordered himself driven back to the marina. He was pleased with himself. The salesman was as full of shit as a Christmas turkey. For one thing, the velocity of .308 Winchester 168-grain soft points was almost precisely that of cartridge, 7.62-mm NATO armor-piercing. For another, if some dummy filed the nose off the AP, the core probably would be shot out of the bullet, leaving the jacket in the barrel. The next time the rifle was fired, the barrel would blow up.

Most important, however, was that he had just replenished his ammunition supply with three hundred rounds of AP, and he hadn't had to provide his name. The creeps from Alcohol, Tobacco and Firearms would not be able to feed his name into their computer for having acquired a "suspicious quantity of military ammunition."

As he walked down the wharf to the *Barbara-Ann*, the pleased feeling vanished instantly. There was somebody aboard, a man in a seersucker suit who had made himself comfortable in one of the deck chairs. There was no question whatever in Hubbard's mind that he was some kind of a cop.

Hubbard stepped from the wharf onto the rear deck. The man in the seersucker suit pushed himself out of the deck chair and, after taking a good look at Hubbard up close, smiled at him. It was the sort of smile given to people who walk onto a used car lot by a salesman who hasn't done well lately.

"Captain Hubbard, I hope?" the man said. He was stocky and florid-faced and was, Hubbard decided, a lot smarter than he looked.

"Who are you, and what are you doing on this boat?" Hubbard asked levelly.

The man walked close to Hubbard and looked down into the shot shell carton full of rifle ammunition. "Target shooting, no doubt?'' he said.

"I got it at a bargain," Hubbard said. "The guy in the store told me that all I have to do is file the tip off and it's just as good, maybe better, than regular ammunition."

"You do that, and you know what'll happen? You'll get your forehead decorated with pieces of blown-up barrel."

"No kidding? You mean it's dangerous? What'll I do with it?"

"Very good." The man laughed. "Yes, I'd say filing the tips off armor-piercing bullets is dangerous to your health." He walked to the window in the cabin and put his little finger in one of the bullet holes. "Not as dangerous to your health as this," he said, "but dangerous."

"That happened when I was parked in a marina," Hubbard said. "Kids, I suppose. Or vandals."

"Sure it was," the man said, mocking him. He walked to Hubbard, showed him two fired 7.62-mm cases he apparently had found on the deck, and dropped then into the carton. "Someone try to liberate your boat, Hubbard?"

"Who the hell are you?" Hubbard asked.

"I'll bet you think I'm a cop."

"That thought ran through my mind until I remembered that only a stupid cop would come on my boat without a search warrant."

"No cop and no warrant," the man said. "If you're going to put that carton inside, I'll be happy to open the door to the cabin for you."

"Open it," Hubbard said. He went inside and sat the carton down on the table. Then he opened the refrigerator and took out two bottles of beer.

"If you're not a cop, then you're not on duty, and you can have a beer, right?"

"I'd have one, thank you, if I were still a cop," the man said, taking one of the bottles from Hubbard. He took a healthy swallow from it. "Thanks," he said. "It was warm out there." He added, "I put in twenty-five years on the force, the last fourteen on the bunco squad in New York."

"And now what do you do?"

"I try to save an insurance company's money," he said. "Much better hours and much better pay. And I get to live in Lauderdale, which is nicer in the winter than Great Neck."

He handed Hubbard a card. It said that his name was James K. Fallon and that he was the chief of the special adjustments division for a major insurance company.

"I'm sorry," Hubbard said. "I seem to be fresh out of cards. What can I do for you, Mr. Fallon? You can start by telling me how you know my name."

"OK," Fallon said after a moment's hesitation. "Mrs. Wood gave your name to the lady next door in case something happened to the little boy. When I told her I was from the insurance company and had to get in touch with Mrs. Wood, she gave it to me. It wasn't hard to find you after that. I'm good at what I do."

"That might have put Mrs. Wood in New Orleans," Hubbard said. "It wouldn't put me here."

"I made a couple of calls to find out who Jack Hubbard was and what Jack Hubbard does for a living," Fallon said. "And then I spent a couple of dimes calling marinas, offering fifty bucks to the first person who called me and told me they had seen the *Barbara-Ann*."

"OK," Hubbard said, deciding that Fallon was telling the truth. He took a pull at his beer. "Now tell me why."

"What else do you think I learned about you when I checked you out?

"That I drink a lot and hate little children and cats?"

"That too," Fallon said, chuckling. "But I told you, I'm very good at what I do. I found out, for example, that despite some rumors to the contrary, you have nothing to do with people from Colombia and that you're very good at what you do, too.''

"What did you hear I do?"

"That for a price, you find things for people," Fallon said.

"They call it marine salvage," Hubbard said.

"Right," Fallon said. "You must do well at it. This is a very nice boat. What did you do, buy it from the government at an auction?"

It was a good guess, Hubbard thought. Vessels engaged in the drug traffic are subject to forfeit when their operators are caught. The vessels are then auctioned off. The drug people show up at the auctions and buy them back, regarding the money as a necessary cost of doing business. But the drug people would not be very interested in buying a boat like the *Barbara-Ann* back when larger and faster vessels were available. A boat like the *Barbara-Ann* could be bought at a bargain price.

"This was a legitimate marine disaster," Hubbard said. "It burned. I bid on it when the insurance company put it up for sale."

"And then you fixed it up?" Fallon asked. "Well, you did a nice job with it, I'll say that."

"Get to the point, will you?"

"All right," Fallon said agreeably. "The policy Mr. Arthur Wood had with our company had a clause that provided that in the event of his demise while he was engaged in a criminal activity, all we have to do is refund the premiums."

"And you think Mr. Wood was engaged in something criminal?"

"What the hell do you think? That he was out there picking up a passenger from a yacht?"

"You tell me."

"Let me put it this way," Fallon said. "If somebody went down and found the airplane and the body and something illegal—probably cocaine; you can hardly get enough grass in a little plane like that to make it worthwhile—that would indicate the late Mr. Wood was involved in a criminal activity at the moment of his unfortunate demise, and my company would not have to write a check for a quarter of a million dollars. Under circumstances like that, my company would be very generous.''

"How generous?''

"The going rate is ten percent.''

"I'm spoken for," Hubbard said. "Sorry.''

"I can't get involved in competitive bidding, you understand," Fallon said. "But I could probably get you another five.''

"Not interested.''

"You mind telling me why?'' Fallon asked.

"I owed Art Wood," Hubbard explained. "I'm paying the debt by bringing up his body.''

"Well, in that case, Captain Hubbard, we don't have anything more to talk about, do we?''

"It doesn't look that way," Hubbard said.

Fallon stared at Hubbard appraisingly.

"Looking for something?'' Hubbard asked.

"I was just trying to figure out what kind of a fool you are," Fallon said. "Whether you're thinking you can crab the cocaine for yourself with me and whoever else knows it's down there watching you or whether you're really fool enough to stick your neck out for a piece of ass.''

"I told you," Hubbard said icily, "I owed Wood. This has nothing to do with his wife.''

"No, of course it doesn't," Fallon said sarcastically. He put his beer bottle carefully on the table and then walked out of the cabin.

CHAPTER

9

Watching the retired New York City detective walk down the wharf, Hubbard decided that Fallon's rudeness, which had reached sort of a pinnacle with the remarks about being dumb and being sexually involved with Laura Wood, had been deliberate. He wanted to make Hubbard angry, since angry men make mistakes. Hubbard was familiar with that technique.

Neither did Hubbard think that Fallon expected him to rush after him, to say he'd take the thirty thousand. What it all added up to was two things. First, that his snap judgment of Fallon had been correct. He was both smarter than he wanted to look and, as he put it, very good at what he did. The second conclusion was that Fallon really believed that Arthur Wood had been up to something illegal, probably transporting narcotics, most likely cocaine.

It was, however, also possible that Fallon was wrong or that he was playing a hunch based on Art Wood's reputation. The offer of the thirty thousand dollars had

had a large hook in it: The insurance company's generosity was contingent on Hubbard's finding something that would relieve them of their double indemnity obligation. The money had not been offered up front.

The thing to do was see just who the man who owned the *Non-Deductible* really was.

Hubbard put the rifle ammunition away and then went back down the wharf to the marina. He found a listing for "Corten, Dexter Real Est" in the telephone book. Then he got into a taxi and ordered himself driven to the address.

The building was very much like others on the street. There were two floors built of concrete block, with a fieldstone facing where it could be seen. There was a well-watered lawn in front of the building with the street number and the legend "Dexter Corten Enterprises." There was a small parking lot in front and a road leading to a larger lot in the rear. There was a neat little sign saying "Mr. Corten" in front of an empty parking space in front. The cars in the adjacent stalls were expensive ones.

A very attractive, large-bosomed blond sat behind a chrome and stainless-steel desk and flashed a large smile at him when he pushed the tinted glass door open and walked into the building.

"May I help you, sir?"

"I'd like to see Mr. Corten," Hubbard said.

"Have you an appointment, sir?" she asked, consulting a notebook on the desk.

"No," Hubbard said. "I wanted to see him about the plane crash."

She looked at him with fresh interest.

"My name is Hubbard," he said. "I've been hired to raise the plane."

She looked at him another moment and then picked up the handset of a multiline telephone set and pushed a button on it.

"Mr. Frazier," she said. "There's a gentleman here I

think you should see." Then she put the handset in its cradle and looked at Hubbard again. "Mr. Corten is out of the office," she said. "Mr. Frazier, our executive vice president, will see you."

Frazier appeared a moment later, a man of Hubbard's age but larger and, Hubbard instantly saw, smoother. He was wearing a light blue suit with a yellow shirt whose collar was open and arranged over the suit jacket collar. His hair was carefully combed, and he wore an expensive watch.

Hubbard wasn't sure which car in the parking lot out front was Frazier's, but it was one or the other. Frazier was not the kind of man who would be driving a jalopy.

"I'm Gerry Frazier," Frazier said to him, putting out his hand. "You wanted to see me?"

"I wanted to see Mr. Corten," Hubbard said. "About the plane crash."

"Well, Mr. Corten's out of the office for the moment, I'm afraid," Frazier said. "But perhaps I can help you."

"Were you on the boat when the crash happened?" Hubbard asked.

"I didn't get your name," Frazier said, still smiling, but far less warmly.

"Hubbard. I've been hired to raise the plane."

"By whom?"

"By Mrs. Arthur Wood."

"Why don't you come into my office?" Frazier asked with a smile, and led Hubbard through a corridor into a large office on the corner of the building.

"Can I get you a cup of coffee or something? A drink?" Frazier asked.

"No, thank you."

"I'm not quite sure what to think. Mrs. Wood hired you, you said?"

"That's right," Hubbard said. "And what I'd like to get from either you or Mr. Corten is some information. What happened. Where the plane is. That sort of thing."

"Frankly, I'm a little surprised at what you tell me," Frazier said. "I happen to know that Mr. Corten is taking care of having the plane raised and recovering Mr. Wood's body."

"Why would he want to do that?"

"I don't think that's really any of your business," Frazier said. "But I can't see where it would do any harm to tell you. Art Wood was in effect an employee of Mr. Corten's when the accident happened. He doesn't have any legal obligation, of course. Technically, Art Wood was an independent contractor, responsible for his own insurance. But Mr. Corten feels a moral obligation. The bottom line is that he was out in the Dry Tortugas because Mr. Corten had hired him to come out there. So Mr. Corten's making arrangements to do what he can to set things right. Specifically, he's contracted with Key West Salvors. You know them?" Hubbard nodded. "To do what has to be done. If it hadn't been for the weather, they'd have already been out there and on their way back."

"Mrs. Wood didn't say anything about this to me," Hubbard said.

"I hope you haven't already gone to a lot of trouble," Frazier said.

"I came across the Gulf from Mississippi," Hubbard said.

"That puts you in a rather awkward position, doesn't it?" Frazier said. "I'm sorry."

"I've had some expenses," Hubbard siad. "You know what fuel costs these days."

"Now that I think of it," Frazier said, "what Mr. Corten is really trying to do is keep Mrs. Wood from spending any money. I'm sure that he'd be willing to reimburse you for your expenses and for your time rather than have you bill Mrs. Wood. Could you give me a ball park figure?"

"I get a thousand dollars a day plus expenses," Hubbard said. "Except for fuel, there haven't been many expenses."

"From Mississippi?" Frazier said. "I'm curious why Mrs. Wood would go all the way to Mississippi to hire a salvage expert."

"I think somebody recommended me to her," Hubbard said.

"Look, why don't you make up a bill and either run it by here or pop it in the mail, and then you can wind this up."

"Mrs. Wood hired me, Mr. Frazier," Hubbard said. "She'll have to fire me."

"That's being a little unreasonable, isn't it? I mean, after all, the poor woman's just lost her husband. You certainly wouldn't want to be accused of taking advantage of her, would you?"

"She may have her own reasons for wanting me to recover the body," Hubbard said. "As I said, she hired me, so she'll have to fire me."

"If you make things difficult for Mrs. Wood, Mr. Hubbard, I don't think Mr. Corten would appreciate it."

"I have no intention of making things difficult for Mrs. Wood," Hubbard said. "You said you were on the boat?"

Frazier took a moment to make sure his temper was under control before he replied, and his reply was simply an affirmative nod.

"What happened?"

"Art brought the plane in for a landing, and on the first or second bounce he hit something. I don't know what. The plane went over on its back, exploded, and sank. There was never a question of doing anything to help him."

"Do you happen to know exactly where you were? Where it sank?"

"We were a couple of miles off to the north of Fort Jefferson," Frazier said. "That guesstimate may be off as much as a half a mile or more."

"There's an insurance adjuster," Hubbard said. "A

man named Fallon. He seems to feel that Mr. Wood was involved in the drug trade."

"I wouldn't know about that," Frazier said. "All I know about Art Wood is that he operated a float plane for charter and that every time we used his service, he was reliable."

"Who exactly was he picking up from your boat?" Hubbard asked.

"That's none of your business, is it?"

"Is there some reason you don't want to tell me?" Hubbard asked.

"OK," Frazier said after a long pause, "I'll tell you. And deny on a stack of Bibles, if I'm ever asked, that I did." He smiled. "From time to time, Mr. Hubbard, Mr. Corten and I need a little relaxation. What Art Wood was doing when the accident happened was to ferry the relaxation back to shore. You'll understand why I don't think the relaxation needs to have names."

"OK," Hubbard said, and smiled back. "I'll tell you what I'm going to do, Mr. Frazier. I'm going to see Mrs. Wood and tell her what you told me. And I'm going to tell her that I think Key West Salvors are among the best in the business. And I'll tell her I'll let her out of the contract if that's what she wants."

"Fine," Frazier said.

"And then I'll send you a bill," Hubbard said. "And you can mail me a check."

"Now that I think about that," Frazier said. "Why don't you just come in here before you start for home? I think Mr. Corten would prefer to pay you in cash. You wouldn't mind cash, would you?"

"Cash would be fine," Hubbard said. He stood up and shook Frazier's hand.

"Call before you come back," Frazier said. "So you won't have to wait when you come here. Can you find your way out?"

"I'll have to call a cab," Hubbard said. "Is there a phone I can use."

"You'll have a hell of a time getting a cab this time of day," Frazier said. "Give me a minute and I'll have somebody run you back to the marina in my car."

"That's very nice," Hubbard said. "Thank you."

Frazier walked him back to the entrance foyer.

"Doris," he said to the good-looking blond, "get Mr. Hubbard a cup of coffee and a magazine and amuse him until I can get Bob up here to run him back to the marina."

"Coffee, tea, or me, Mr. Hubbard?" the blond said, smiling at him as if he were an old friend.

Hubbard's coffee barely had time to cool to a drinkable temperature before a pleasant-looking young man in glasses came into the reception area and announced that he was Bob. Any time Hubbard was ready, he was ready to run him by the marina.

Hubbard took the coffee with him. He told the blond that he would return the cup with Bob. She told him to come back real soon. Bob had a station wagon, and Hubbard sensed that the car was owned by the company for precisely the purpose to which it now was being put.

Bob was a pleasant young man who made amusing idle conversation as he drove Hubbard directly back to the marina. Hubbard found that very interesting, for he hadn't told anyone where he had docked the *Barbara-Ann*.

He thanked Bob for the ride, and Bob smiled and drove away.

He started down the wharf to the *Barbara-Ann*, wondering whether Laura Wood would be waiting for him when he got there or whether he would have to wait for her. He wondered what he would tell her when he saw her.

The story Frazier had told him was credible not because he thought that Dexter Corten was at all concerned with Wood's widow but because Corten would be concerned with having it become public knowledge that he and Frazier had been out in the Dry Tortugas with a couple of bimbos.

The oblique reference to sex brought to Hubbard's mind's eye an image of Laura Wood's erect nipples when he had bandaged the cut on her breast, and that image was quickly replaced with the image of her innocently exposing her breasts again when she had knelt on the foredeck while taking the line from the hatch. He experienced a nearly forgotten chill. The skin on his back seemed to crawl, and a foul acid seemed to crawl up his throat. He realized that he was holding his breath, and he forced himself to exhale. The air he forced from his throat made him grunt weakly.

And I left the goddamn .38 in the cabin.

He forced himself to keep walking, and then he forced a smile on his face as he turned around to see who was following him, to see if what his instincts told him was true or whether the alarm had been triggered by something innocent, someone from another boat getting onto the walkway.

There were two men, dark-haired, in slacks and sports shirts worn outside the trousers. The one closest to him was crouched, and he had his arms extended. His right hand held a knife. And it was a *knife*, Hubbard saw, not a switchblade but a dagger, a fighting knife, probably a Fairbairn, and he was holding it as if he knew exactly how to use it.

"I won't give you any trouble," Hubbard said. "No trouble at all. Please don't hurt me."

The man made a "give me" motion by moving the fingers of his left hand.

Hubbard held his hands out in front of himself defensively, as if to ward off the strike of the knife. Then he turned as if to run. The man with the knife lunged after him, but by then Hubbard had spun on the ball of his foot so that he was in a position to grab the man's wrist and twist it. When the man fell to the pier, the weight of his body tore the ball of his arm from the shoulder socket. He groaned as he fell on the wharf. Hubbard scurried on his knees to get the knife. When he had it in his hand, he jumped to his feet in a crouching position.

The other man had a switchblade knife in his hand, and he was frantically trying to take something, almost certainly a pistol, from the small of his back. Hubbard rushed him, feinting with the knife in his right hand and then using the stiff, pressed together fingers of his left hand to stab him in the larynx. The force of the lunge was sufficient to knock the man over backward. But as he fell, he managed to free a revolver. Hubbard stamped at the hand holding the gun with his heel. The man's arm jerked in an involuntary defensive movement, and the revolver came free and went flying through the air and into the water. The man now had both hands at his bruised and perhaps crushed larynx. The thumb and index finger of the hand that had held the gun were broken, with the thumb hanging back over the wrist and the index finger hanging limply and crookedly from the first knuckle.

The man was turning blue. Hubbard raised his foot and aimed at the man's face. Terrified, wide-eyed, the man moved his hands to protect his face. Hubbard changed the direction of the kick to his abdomen, and at the last second before contact stopped the blow and converted it to a healthy shove. Sometimes that worked and sometimes it didn't. It depended on how much damage you had done to the throat and larynx. This time it worked. There was a grunting sound of expelled air as an air passage was opened. Then the man grunted again, a frightened, frightening animal sound of fear and anguish.

He scurried backward away from Hubbard, pushing himself with frantic movements of his legs until he backed into one of the telephone-pole-size pilings. Hubbard, again in a knife-fighting crouch, moved past him so that his back was toward the *Barbara-Ann*. He glanced at the man who had first attacked him. He was rolling in pain on the wharf, his left hand holding the right arm near the dislocated shoulder.

"Get him out of here," Hubbard said to the man in front of him. He gestured with the knife. The man, his breath coming in painful heaves, nodded his head as if in agreement but didn't move.

"I don't want to have to kill you," Hubbard said. There was something close to an entreaty in his voice.

The man got first to his knees and then, halfway to the second man, got unsteadily to his feet. With a good deal of effort, he got the second man to his feet and, supporting him, led him down the wharf.

Hubbard stayed in the crouched fighting position until they had gone out of sight. Then, very slowly, he stood erect. He looked at the hand holding the knife as if it were something he had never seen before. The hand and arm started to tremble. He put the other hand to the wrist and tried to quell the shaking. Then he ran down the pier, still holding his wrist with the other hand, and jumped into the *Barbara-Ann*'s cockpit.

He went to the cabin door and leaned on his right arm, the hand of which still held the knife against it. With his left hand, he pulled a necklace from inside his shirt and, after some fumbling, got the key it held into the lock. He pulled the key out, opened the door, stumbled inside, and then bolted the door.

He walked unsteadily across the cabin and sat down heavily on the couch. He exhaled noisily and seemed to be looking at the carpet. Then he seemed to become aware of the knife in his hand. He relaxed his white-knuckled grip on it and held it in the palm of his hand. It was a Fairbairn, all right, a genuine Fairbairn. A new one, one of the "commemoratives," engraved with the date of the British commando raid on Dieppe and a commando strip. Hubbard remembered seeing them advertised for a hundred and fifty dollars.

The man who had tried to use this knife on him, he decided, had not been a collector of military paraphernalia. He had been a professional who paid whatever the market demanded for the tools of his trade. He leaned over to lay the knife on the table beside the couch and suddenly smelled himself.

"Jesus Christ," he said in repugnance. It was a smell which like that of decaying human bodies was distinctive and unforgettable. It was the smell of terror, of the human reduced by fear for his life to an animal. He got to his feet and went to the master's cabin. He came back out immediately and took the Smith & Wesson Model 36 snubnose from the drawer where he had left it. Then he put it under a towel on the washstand by the shower. He stripped off his clothes, leaving them in a heap on the floor, and stepped into the shower.

CHAPTER
10

Hubbard showered until the water turned cold and then stayed under the cold water until he was chilled. Then he stepped out of the shower. As he was toweling his hair, he sensed movement on the boat. He wrapped the towel around his waist and reached under the towel on the washbasin and picked up the snubnose .38.

I'm getting the damned thing wet, he thought with annoyance. Now I'll have to clean it.

He went to the door of the master's cabin and slid the locking latch open. He carefully cocked the hammer of the revolver and then, holding the pistol in front of him with both hands at the level of his shoulders, kicked the door open.

Laura Wood was on the aft deck, facing away from the cabin. He was relieved that she hadn't seen him holding the pistol on her like a television supercop. He pulled the door closed and took a pair of khaki pants from a drawer and slipped them on. He went out through the cabin and unlocked the cabin door.

"I wasn't sure you were here," she said.

"I was taking a shower," he informed her.

"I'm sorry I took so long," she said.

"I went to see Dexter Corten."

"You did?" She was surprised.

"He wasn't there," Hubbard told her. "But a man named Frazier told me that Corten's hired a salvage operator, Key West Salvors. I know them, and they're good. And that I'm not needed anymore."

"Mr. Frazier," Laura said, "is Mr. Corten's alter ego." Then, as if thinking aloud, she asked: "Why would he want to do that?"

"Frazier says that he, Corten, feels a moral obligation. Because your husband was working for him at the time."

"Do you believe that?" Laura asked.

"Not for a minute," he said. "And when Frazier saw that, he came up with another story."

"What was that?"

"That he and Corten had a couple of women out there and that what Art was doing was picking them up. Quietly."

"I think that could be true," she said.

"So do I," he said. "He offered to pay me what you have paid me so far, and he didn't blink an eyelash when I told him I get a thousand a day and expenses. I guess if you have either a reputation to maintain or a jealous and/or suspicious wife, you have to expect to pay."

"What did you tell him?"

"That I would tell you what he told me," Hubbard said, "and let you make the decision."

"What decision?"

"Whether you want me to back out of this and let Corten take care of you."

"I came back here deciding to say something to you," Laura said. "Now I wonder if you'll believe that I was going to say this before you told me what you just did."

"What's that?" Hubbard asked.

"You might think you owe Jack something," she said. "But you don't owe me anything. I want to pay you. When I get the insurance company's check, I mean."

"There's more," Hubbard said. "There may not be an insurance check."

"What?" she asked, surprised and a little frightened.

"An insurance adjuster was here. A man named Fallon. He offered me twenty-five thousand dollars if I brought up proof that your husband was doing something illegal—what he means is drugs—so they won't have to pay off on the insurance."

She looked at him with her eyebrows raised. "Is that what this is all about?" she asked. "You know I can't match an offer like that."

"I turned him down," Hubbard said. Then, crazily, he heard himself adding, "Money's not what I want from you."

She looked at him in surprise, and he saw understanding in her eyes.

"What exactly," she asked levelly, "do you want from me?"

"That didn't come out the way I intended," he said.

"How was it intended to come out?" she said, on the edge of anger.

"What I meant to say was there's not enough money around to get me involved in something like this. If you tried to hire me, you couldn't afford me, and neither could Fallon, much less Corten with a lousy five thousand."

"I thought you did this kind of thing for a living," Laura said.

"That's the key word," Hubbard replied, " 'living.' I try very hard not to get involved in things where people are likely to try to kill me, and if I guess wrong and find myself involved in something where somebody tries to kill me, then I run."

"You're talking about what happened on the way down here?"

"I'm talking about what happened here, thirty minutes ago, on the dock."

"What are you talking about?" she asked.

"When I came back from trying to see Corten, there were two guys waiting for me. They tried to stick knives in me."

She looked at him in disbelief and then saw proof in his eyes. She felt a chill down her back.

"What happened?"

"I was lucky," he said. "You can see that."

"Are you hurt?"

"No," he said. "Scared but not hurt."

"Who were they?"

"I don't know," he said. "I wish I did."

"I have no reason to distrust Dexter Corten," she told him. "If he says he's going to raise the airplane, he'll do it."

"Dexter Corten may get Art's body, and he might not," Hubbard said. "Or the insurance guy may get out there first with his divers, and if your husband was carrying cocaine or something—"

"There was nothing on that airplane," she said, interrupting, "I vacuumed it just before he left."

"We don't know that he crashed on landing," Hubbard said.

"What do you mean?"

"Let's suppose that he crashed on takeoff, after he'd picked up the bimbos and an attaché case full of cocaine."

She looked at him.

"You think he was dealing in drugs, don't you?"

"Yes," he said. "I think he was. Which means that Corten is probably involved. Which means that Corten wants to recover them from the plane. Which explains this generosity of his. He can look like Mr. Nice Guy while some diver for Key West Salvors is looking for his property. If I'm nosing around out there, I'm liable to find them first. And since Fallon thinks there are drugs down there, that means he'll be trying to recover them too, to beat you out of the insurance money."

"So what do you think I should do?" Laura asked.

"That's the decision you're going to have to make," Hubbard told her. "Whether you want to let Corten recover the body, in which case I will bow out of the whole thing, or whether you want me to do what you asked me to do."

Laura looked into his eyes so intently and for so long that Hubbard was made very uncomfortable.

"Do you have to look at me that way?" he asked.

"I guess I was trying to figure you out," Laura confessed.

"Don't try," he said.

"I think I'll stick with you," she said, making up her mind.

"OK," Hubbard said.

"What are we going to do now?"

"What am *I* going to do?" Hubbard corrected her. "The only chance I have is to get out there and find the body first."

"I stand corrected," Laura said.

"Do you have to tell anybody you've left?" he asked.

"No."

"Go forward and let loose the lines," he told her, and pushed past her and went up the ladder to the controls on the upper deck.

They were ten miles down the Caloosahatchee River from Fort Myers when Hubbard turned to Laura and said, "We're approaching that housing development or whatever it is we passed on the way up the river."

"Cape Coral," she said.

"Is there a hotel or something there where you could stay?" he asked.

"I don't understand."

"Or you can stay with Tony Pombal's wife," he said. "That would probably be better."

"If you didn't want me along, why didn't you leave me in Fort Myers?" Laura asked.

"I thought it would be better if you were someplace you'd be hard to find," he explained.

"I want to go out there with you," she said. "Anyway, you said you wanted to get out there as soon as you could. You don't have to go back through Pine Island Sound to get into the Gulf. You can go around either end of Sanibel Island. Going back to Port Boca Grande would take another two hours at least."

"You weren't listening to me before," he said. "I told you, two men tried to kill me while you were gone. I don't know who they were, but they knew their business. I think it's very likely they'll try it again. You've got no business out where we're going."

"So you want to drop me off?"

"Obviously, that's the thing to do."

"No way," she said.

"You'll be in the way," he said.

"I'm going, Jack," she said firmly.

"Is that fair to your kid?"

"My kid is my business," she said. "Nobody else's."

He looked into her eyes. She met his gaze unflinchingly.

"OK?" she asked. After a moment, Hubbard nodded.

"Do you want something to eat?" Laura asked.

"In one of the cabinets," Hubbard said, "there's a do-it-yourself fried chicken thing. You know how to work one?"

"Is there an instruction manual?"

"There's a drawer full of manuals, lowest drawer on the right," he said.

"Then I can work it," she said.

While the chicken was cooking, she opened cans of potatoes and made potato salad. Then, with five minutes still to go before the chicken would be done, she went to the head. She saw his discarded clothing on the deck and picked it up. It was sweat-soaked, and she held it away from her. Then she gave into a perverse urge to smell it. The smell was absolutely foul and nearly made her gag.

She had seen the washing machine built into the cabinetry beside the dishwasher. She pulled the door down and found a box of soap flakes inside. She put his foul clothes in the machine, added soap, and turned it on. By then, the chicken was done. She burned her finger slightly as the hot fat sloshed around from the movement of the boat. She put it in her mouth and sucked on it. She saw her reflection in a mirror. She studied herself in the mirror.

When he asked if my going with him was fair to Little Art, she thought, I really didn't think that through before I ran off at the mouth. Why the hell is it so important to me not to be left behind, which is another way of saying why is it so important to me to be with him?

She remembered reading somewhere that widows and other women who had lost their men often made asses of themselves with other men, that there was something about losing one man than made women throw themselves at the nearest male.

Is that what's happening to me?

More important, can Jack Hubbard sense it? That remark about what he wants from me is not money was a slip on his part, no matter how firmly he denied it.

The absolute bottom line is that I really wish he would put his arms around me and tell me that everything's going to be all right. Is that the lonely widow looking for solace wherever she can find it, or do I just have the hots for Jack Hubbard?

In either case, I will not let anything happen. The one thing I don't need right now is to get involved with a man, especially a man like Jack Hubbard.

He is, she reminded herself, a man with an unsavory reputation who was in jail and who lives with the madam of a whorehouse. All I have to do is keep reminding myself of that.

They had left Fort Myers at half past three in the afternoon. At half past two the next morning, Laura, who had been sleeping in her clothes on the bed in the master stateroom, was wakened by a change in the pitch of the boat and its engines. She felt the *Barbara-Ann* slow and a minute or two after felt her shudder as the engines revved and Hubbard put the transmission in reverse. A moment after that, she heard the dull rumble of the anchor chain.

The vibration of the diesels died, and then there came the sound of a smaller engine starting, running roughly for a moment or two, and then smoothing down. After a moment, she realized that he had started the auxiliary power generator.

She knew that Hubbard was now coming down from the upper deck. She wondered whether she could somehow sense that movement or whether she "knew" because coming down from the upper deck was the thing he would now obviously do.

She got out of bed and walked into the cabin as he came into it from the cockpit.

"Where are we?"

"Off Fort Jefferson," he said.

"Do you want something to eat?" she asked.

"I think I'd rather have a beer," he said. He went to the couch and lay down on it. She had just opened the refrigerator when he said, "I think I'll make that a drink."

"I'll get it for you," she said.

"Do you think you could stay awake for the rest of the night?" Hubbard asked. "For a couple of hours at least?"

"I've been sleeping," she said. "I can stay awake."

She put ice cubes and water in a glass and handed him

one of the half-gallon bottles of bourbon.

"Thank you," he said. He looked tired, and she told him so.

"A little," he admitted. He poured a stiff shot of bourbon on top of the iced water and then sipped at it.

"I haven't said thank you for helping me," she said.

"Save your breath," he said. "I'm out here because I have to be."

"What do you mean by that?"

"Didn't you hear what I told you before?" he asked, his voice sounding as tired as he looked. "Two guys, two professionals, tried to kill me." He reached over to the couchside table and picked up the Fairbairn knife. "With this," he said, and held it up. She took a couple of steps toward him, and he handed it to her.

"It looks like something that should be mounted in a glass case and hung on a living room wall," Laura said.

"That's a Fairbairn," he said. "A real one. From Wilkinson sword. It's a commemorative, made to sell to people to hang on walls, but it's just as good as the plain model. More pople have been killed by professionals with knives like that than with any other. Fairbairn was a Shanghai cop who taught the commandos how to use a knife. We got it from the English via the First Special Forces Group. It's been around a long time."

"Who's we?" she asked.

"The American military," he informed her. "The unconventional American military."

"Like the Green Berets, you mean?"

"And the SEALS, and the Air Commandos, which are the Air Force's answer to the SEALS, which are the Navy's answer to the Green Berets."

"You liked being a SEAL, didn't you?" she asked. "Despite everything?"

"Yeah," he said after a moment. "I did."

"Is that why you're helping me?" she asked. The thought had just then occurred to her. "For the thrill? The excitement?"

He looked at her in utter disbelief. Then he chuckled,

and the chuckles gave way to laughter. Through the laughter he said, "Oh, Jesus Christ!"

"What's so funny?" she snapped.

"I'm helping you for two reasons," he said. "One of which is that, for the fifth or sixth time, I owed your husband."

And what's the other one? That maybe you've heard the stories about how easy it is to get into a widow's pants by offering her a broad masculine chest to lean against? Sure you have, you bastard. That remark about what you want from me not being money was not innocent.

"And the other one?" she asked.

He looked at her a moment before replying: "Because I learned a long time ago that when somebody you don't know tries to kill you, the worst thing you can do is run. A man who doesn't know where he's running or from what is a very easy man to take out."

"And you think," she asked, "that whoever it was is going to come out here?"

"If they do," he said, "then I'll know who they are. Right now I don't."

"You didn't tell me exactly what happened," Laura said.

"I thought I did," he said, and then went on: "I was walking down the wharf, back to the *Barbara-Ann*. And right there in the bright sunlight, I began to stink."

"I don't know what that means," Laura said.

"An animal senses danger," he explained. "Instinctively. And when that happens, something happens to the body. It makes people stink."

Uncomfortably, she remembered the foul odor of the clothing he had dropped on the cabin floor.

"Something like the smell of rut," he said. "When the veneer of civilization cracks and falls off, we behave like the animals we are."

"That's not very pleasant to think about it, is it?" she said as much to herself as to him as she considered that the widow throwing herself into the arms of the next available male was an animal reaction.

"It kept me alive this afternoon," he said matter-of-factly.

"What exactly happened?"

"When I turned around and took a look," he said, "there were two guys behind me on the wharf. When they saw me looking, they came after me."

And then what happened? Laura wondered impatiently, wanting him to get on with the story. What happened to the men? If there were trying to kill you, why didn't they? What did you do to them? And then she found her own answer, at once incredible and logical.

"So you killed them?" she asked, the words sounding unreal in her ears even as she looked at Jack Hubbard and knew that he was perfectly capable of killing people and not being particularly upset by it.

"No," he said, again shaking his head at what he obviously thought to be her gross stupidity. He looked at her and offered an explanation: "I didn't want to find myself explaining two bodies to the Fort Myers cops. They have a law against killing people."

Well, I was right about him not worrying about the moral questions of taking a human life, she thought. If it wouldn't have been inconvenient for him, he would have killed and thought nothing about it. If I know that about him, she wondered, why is it that I'm not afraid of him?

"If they were trying to kill you," Laura said, "and you had the knife to prove it, couldn't you have told the police it was self-defense?"

"You've been watching too many TV movies," he said. "This is the real world. If I had taken those guys out, I would have spent the next six months and a hell of a lot of money trying to stay out of jail. And if I went up before a judge who didn't believe in any amount of bail for capital cases and sent me to jail to wait for the wheels of justice to grind, some friends of theirs would have shoved a sharpened bed spring between my ribs.''

"But otherwise you would have killed them?" Laura asked softly.

What my attraction for this man is, is nothing more than morbid curiosity. Talking to him is like gaping at a bloody traffic accident. There is some kind of a thrill.

"What I would have liked to have done was get one of them somewhere where I could have asked him who sent them," he said.

"You think he would have told you?" Laura asked.

"He would have told me," Hubbard said flatly.

God, there he goes again. That was so menacing, it was thrilling.

"Who do you think they were?" she asked.

"I've been thinking about that," he said. "Unless, of course, I missed and took out somebody on that boat off Panama City, and I'm up against a South American Latin vendetta, I don't think it was friends of the people on that boat. For one thing, unless they just happened to see us come up the river, how would they have known where to find me?"

"Then who?"

"We get back to drugs," Hubbard said. "Down here, everything is involved with drugs. God damn him, any-way."

"God damn who?" Laura asked.

Hubbard looked at her. There was no question that he was talking about Art.

"How'd you get tied up with him?" Hubbard asked.

"Probably the same way you got hung up with Bar-bara-Ann," Laura said. "He wasn't what he appeared to be."

"Touché," he said after a moment.

"You asked for it," she said.

Hubbard drained his drink and then picked up the half-gallon bottle of bourbon and filled the glass half full again.

CHAPTER
11

"The most likely explanation," Hubbard said after a moment, "is the obvious one. Someone doesn't want me to find the airplane. If it wasn't for the Coast Guard finding debris, I wouldn't be entirely sure there was an airplane."

"I don't understand that at all," Laura said.

"I'm just thinking off the top of my head," Hubbard explained. "And I'm not very good at that."

"Let's hear it," Laura said.

"The figures boggle the mind," he said. "Do you know how much cocaine they can move in an attaché case? I mean, how many dollars worth?"

"A lot," she said. "Millions of dollars worth."

"And the drug people steal from each other," Hubbard told her. "All the time. So let's suppose that somebody stole some here."

"I don't follow you."

"Let's suppose that the reason they don't want me looking for the airplane is because when I do find it, there won't be any drugs on it. Because somebody stole them and then arranged for the crash."

"That seems pretty far-fetched," she said.

"They do some pretty far-fetched things," he told her.

"But that would mean Art was murdered," Laura said.

"For these people, murder is simply a way of doing business," Hubbard said. "So what have we got? Scenario one is that there is something, probably cocaine, in the airplane. Whoever knows that wants to come out here himself and recover it and wanted to get me out of the way. That makes sense. Scenario two is that there's something else in that airplane, something somebody doesn't want recovered, period, like, for example, an empty attaché case that's supposed to be full of cocaine. Or money."

"And scenario three," Laura said, "is that there is nothing on that plane but Art's body, and that's all there ever was, and that everything happened just like Mr. Corten said it did."

"That's possible," Hubbard said.

"But that doesn't explain what happened to you on the wharf," Laura said, shooting down her own theory. "I just can't understand that. Weren't they afraid they'd get caught? Can you murder people and get away with it?"

"It happens all the time," Hubbard said. "If they had killed me, all it would have meant was a small paragraph on page 34 of the newspaper: 'New Orleans Man Killed in Marina Mugging.' "

"The police don't investigate?"

"Not much," Hubbard said. "Murder is common down here. Miami has the highest murder rate in the country. I don't suppose Fort Myers is far behind. And once the cops had checked me out, they wouldn't have bothered to do much about it. I'm the kind of guy who gets killed in a 'mugging.' "

"Why do you say that?" she asked.

"I'm an ex-con," he said. "I did thirty-three months of a five- to fifteen-year sentence at Raiford."

"What's Raiford?"

"The Florida correction facility for men," Hubbard said.

"What did you do?"

"I failed to kill my wife and her lover," he said. "All they could get me for was attempted murder."

"If you didn't kill them," she said, "you didn't want to."

"I wanted to," he said. "I was just a little too drunk to carry it off."

He was serious, and she didn't want to face that. She said the first thing that came into her mind. "I didn't think ex-convicts were permitted to own guns."

"Guns?" he asked, not understanding her for a moment. Then he shook his head in agreement. "The penalty is ten and ten. Ten years and ten thousand dollars. Technically, I'm not an ex-con. The guns are legal. If I go to jail, it won't be on a federal firearms charge.

When he saw the question on her face, he went on: "An admiral I once worked for, who had the old-fashioned notion that wives should not sleep with other men, waved my service record in the governor's face and got me a pardon. The admiral told me the governor said he did it to prove that it's not always true that all a medal and fifty cents will get you is a cup of coffee. But so far as the cops are concerned, and the Coast Guard, and the rest of the law enforcement community, I'm an ex-con. And they're right, of course. Once a man has done time, hard time, he's different."

He met her eyes and then looked away.

"It's the animal thing again," he said. "Man is an animal, and animals are not supposed to live in cages. You ever look, really look, at the animals in a zoo?"

"I'm sorry for you, Jack," Laura said, and without thinking about it, reached out and touched his hand with hers. He recoiled as if her hand had burned him.

"There's something else you should know," he said. "Don't misunderstand me, I'll give it my best shot. But our chances of finding that airplane out here are about one in a hundred, maybe two hundred."

"We know pretty well where he crashed," she protested.

"Don't tell me my business," he said. "What I would need to have any reasonable chance of finding it in forty feet of water is the chart the Coast Guard made when they came out here. They'd have the oil slick marked on it, and the time, and the location of debris, and things like that. Maybe, working from that, I could find it. But there's no way in the world they'd turn it over to me. You need a license to go salvaging. No license, no chart."

"Why didn't you get one?"

"I've been down that street," he said. "The law says they have to issue a license, but it doesn't say how quickly. When an ex-con applies for one, it takes a long time for the bureaucracy to move."

"What's what you need look like?" Laura asked.

"Like any other marine chart," he said. He obviously had no idea why she was asking.

Laura got up and walked into the master's cabin. She came out in a minute and handed Hubbard the Coast and Geodic Survey chart that the Coast Guard chief had just about told her to steal.

"Like this?" she asked. "Is this what you need?"

Hubbard stood up and laid the chart out on the table.

"Where did you get this?" he asked, surprised, seeing that it was marked with just the information he'd been talking about, that it was in fact precisely what he needed.

"I stole it," she said. "When I came out here right after Art crashed. The old chief, the one who gave me your name, made it pretty clear that he wanted me to. Is it what you need?"

"Our chances of finding that plane have just gone up

to maybe fifty-fifty," he said. "And we have this information, and nobody else who wants to find that plane will. At least not yet. It takes a week for something like this to work its way through the bureaucracy."

He smiled at her. When he smiled, she thought, he changed completely.

"It'll help?" she asked.

"Yeah," he said. "Give me a little daylight to orient myself with this and I can start looking." He walked to the rear deck and spent a couple of minutes there, looking around.

"It's too dark now," he said. "I thought it would be. What I need to do is get some sleep. Do you think you could stay awake?"

"Sure," she said. "What am I supposed to be looking for?"

"I'll show you," he said. "Come here."

He led her to the controls and threw some switches. There was the whirring sound of an electric motor, and then the cathode-ray tube of the radar scope began to glow.

"These are the islands," he said, pointing to glowing uneven green marks on the screen. "They won't move. I've got it set on twenty miles. That's the outer ring, you see?"

She nodded.

"Now, all you have to do is watch for something approaching that outer ring. That'll be something headed in this direction."

"How long would it take a boat to get here if I saw one coming?" Laura asked.

"Twenty miles divided by how fast the boat's moving. This is a little too far out for speedboats. Boats this size generally make fourteen, fifteen knots. A fast one, maybe twenty. So the radar gives us an hour, maybe more, as a warning."

"I can handle that," Laura said. "Go take a shower and go to bed."

"Wake me when it's light," he said.

"Right," she said.

Hubbard nodded at her and then went into the master's cabin and closed the door after him. A moment later, she heard the sound of an electric motor and decided it was the sound of the pump sending water to the shower. She walked to the couch, picked up his unfinished drink, and sipped at it. She heard the electric pump motor stop. She looked at radar repeater, watching the sweep of the search circle and circle. She looked at the clock on the control console and waited until the sweep second hand had made a complete sweep from thirty-five past the minute back to thirty-five.

Then she got up and walked to the door of the master's cabin and stepped inside. Hubbard sat up immediately, pulling a sheet over his middle. She was reminded that he slept in the nude. She remembered the last time she'd seen him in bed.

"Something on the screen?" Hubbard asked.

"There's nothing on the radar," Laura said.

"Then what?" Hubbard asked.

"According to you," Laura said, her voice husky despite a valiant effort to keep it light, "that means we have an hour. This shouldn't take more than a couple of minutes."

She reached down and pulled the terrycloth shirt over her head. She didn't look at him when she dropped it on the deck or until she had slid her pants down off her hips and stepped out of them.

What am I going to do if he tells me to put my clothes on and get out of here?

She forced herself to raise her head to look at him. She saw that he was unlikely to reject her. There was a tent in the sheet over his middle. As she walked toward the bed, he threw the sheet off and crawled down the bed toward her. They met awkwardly, but in just a moment or two all the various parts had been properly aligned and set into motion.

*   *   *

"Jesus!" Hubbard exhaled.

"Jesus meaning what?" Laura asked. Hubbard was lying spent on his back, his hands under his head. Laura was lying half on him.

"When I saw you standing there like the ace of spades," Hubbard said, "I realized that I wanted you from the moment you walked into Caroline's apartment."

"Thank you," she said, and then she understood what he meant by "the ace of spades" and laughed deep in her throat and pinched the soft flesh above his hip. "Ace of spades!"

"But that wasn't the smartest thing either of us could have done," Hubbard added.

"Maybe it was inevitable," Laura said.

"Absolutely inevitable," he said. "Every time I get my ass in a crack, I get very horny, and you, you're . . ." he stopped.

"I'm what?"

"Forget it," he said.

"Tell me," she demanded, pushing herself off him enough so that she could look down at his face. He took advantage of the opportunity to get out of bed.

"Tell me," she repeated to his back as he went into the head.

He didn't answer, and the door closed after him. He came out and picked his trousers off the deck and put them on. He looked at her.

"I'm going to have a look at the radar," he said.

"Don't tell me," she said furiously, "that your conscience is bothering you!"

He looked at her and then laughed at her and then walked out of the cabin. If she had had something, she would have thrown it at him.

She rolled onto her back and lay there a while, until she smelled herself and knew that, bandage or not, she was going to have to have a shower. She looked down at her breast. The bandage was loose, nearly off, and she pulled gently on it until it came completely off. The breast was still black and blue, but the wound that had so frightened her was already starting to scab over. She was afraid to get it wet, however, and wondered whether she could take a shower without getting it wet.

There was nothing to do but try.

When she came out of the shower, she half expected him to be there, and for that reason she had draped a towel modestly around her waist and held her hands modestly over her breasts. He would, she figured, not displeased by the thought, have to put another bandage on her.

But he was not in the cabin, which annoyed her, and when he didn't come back into it, she decided that he wasn't going to. He was watching the radar or had worked up an appetite and was making himself something to eat. She was going to have to go out there if she wanted her breast bandaged. She would get him to bandage her breast, and then she would make him something to eat. The thought pleased her; it offered a certain opportunity.

Instead of dressing again in her terrycloth blouse and pants, Laura went through the drawers in a cabinet until she found one of his blue denim work shirts, worn soft and faded by many washings. She put it on, rolled up the sleeves, and then buttoned the middle buttons. She examined herself in the mirror and rather liked what she saw. It was at once, she thought, feminine and sexy. It would tantalize his imagination without being indecent. She wondered if it had been as violently explosive for him as it had been for her. She went back in the head and brushed her hair and looked at her face in the mirror. She looked, she thought, all right.

Then she went out into the cabin. He was standing in midcabin, holding a coffee cup in his hand.

His eyebrows went up when he saw how she was dressed, but he said nothing.

"Where's the first aid kit?" Laura asked. "The bandage came off."

Hubbard pointed with the coffee cup to the first aid kit on the bulkhead.

Damn. Is he going to make me bandage it myself?

She went to the first aid kit, took it off its mount, carried it to the table behind him, and opened it. She took out a roll of adhesive tape and a bandage in an envelope. She tore the envelope open.

"You want some help with that?" Hubbard asked.

"If it wouldn't be too much trouble," Laura said sarcastically.

He walked to her.

"You want to unbutton your shirt?" he said. She unbuttoned the shirt. He looked dispassionately at her breast.

"My doctor said you did a good job," she said.

"He give you a tetanus shot?"

"A tetanus shot and some penicillin pills."

He took the aerosol bottle of antiseptic from the first aid kit and sprayed her carefully again. Then he ripped open the bandage envelope and placed the bandage over the wound and finally taped it in place.

He looked into her eyes.

"If it was your intention to turn me on by coming out here wearing my shirt and nothing else," Hubbard said, "you succeeded."

"I'm glad," she said softly.

Hubbard put his hands on her waist under the open denim shirt and pulled her to him. There was proof that she had indeed turned him on.

"I just hope you understand what's turned you on," he said to the top of her head.

"What would that be?" Laura asked.

"You're a lonely lady," he said, "a frightened, lonely lady. And you think I'm Sir Somebody who can save you from the dragon."

"What's wrong with that?" Laura asked. "From your point of view, I mean?"

He pushed her away from him and looked down at her. He let his hand run down her chest to her unbandaged breast. When the balls of his fingers touched her nipple, it grew erect. Then he caught both sides of her open shirt and started to close the buttons.

"What happened in there took a little longer than you figured it would," he said, and nodded over her shoulder at the radar scope. She turned to follow his glance.

She saw that there were now two new blips on it that hadn't been there before, to their rear, on an area of the scope that reflected what was on the open Gulf of Mexico.

"They're headed this way," he said. "One is about a mile behind the other one. They're making about fifteen knots."

She turned to look at him.

"Who do you think they are?" Laura asked.

"One of them is probably Fallon," Hubbard said. "I haven't the faintest idea about the other. Maybe Corten. We'll just have to wait to see."

"What do we do?"

"Unless they suddenly start to fly," he said, "they can't be here in less than forty-five minutes or an hour."

Oh.

"So unless you want to get laid again, lady, you better put some clothes on," he said.

"I've had more politely phrased offers," Laura said faintly but angrily.

"I'm not going to give you the chance to accuse me of taking advantage of you," Hubbard said.

"You really don't trust women, do you?" Laura asked, as much to herself as to Hubbard.

"Not very far," he said, "and then only very rarely."

"Tell me about Caroline," Laura said.

"Caroline is none of your business," Hubbard said. "Christ, I screw you once, and already you try to stake a claim."

"If you want to get laid again, you're going to have to tell me about her," Laura said.

For a moment, she thought she had gone too far. But then he smiled and shook his head, almost in admiration.

"There's more to you than meets the eye, isn't there?" he said.

"And I also want to know exactly what it is you think you owed Art," Laura insisted.

"Are you willing to wait?" Hubbard asked.

"Wait for what?" she asked, and then she knew what he meant.

"Sure," she said, meeting his eyes. "For all I know, you're an honest man. And you've got no place to get away from me out here."

He looked at her and after a moment smiled. "Now that that's settled," he said, "why don't you unbutton that shirt again?"

"Why don't you?" Laura replied.

CHAPTER
12

When Hubbard came back into the cabin and looked at the radar screen, the two blips, still about a mile from each other, were five miles closer than they had been the last time he looked. That confirmed his estimate of their speed. Five miles in twenty minutes, which was how long he'd been in the bed with Laura, translates to fifteen knots.

Laura, again wearing nothing but his denim shirt, came into the cabin.

"Are you hungry?" she asked. "I'm starved."

"Me, too," he said.

"Ham and eggs or steak and eggs?"

"Steak and eggs," he said.

"I can't imagine," she said sarcastically, "where I got this appetite."

"Which do you want first?" Hubbard asked.

Laura looked at him in confusion and then understood what he was asking.

"Forget it, Jack," she said. "I was just being a bitch. None of that is any of my business."

"I always pay my debts," he said. "Which?"

She met his eyes, looked away, and shrugged her shoulders.

"OK," she said. "Tell me what you owed my husband."

"My life," he said.

She hadn't expected anything so dramatic as that, and she looked at him in surprise.

"We were working up river, on one of the branches of the Mekong River."

"In Vietnam, you mean?"

"Yeah. We were maybe thirty miles into Cambodia."

"Doing what?" she asked.

"The Vietcong were taxing river traffic," Hubbard said. "So we were taking out their tax collectors."

She now knew what he meant by taking out and felt a little chill.

"Art was involved in something like that?"

"He was a Huey pilot," Hubbard said. "Didn't you know?"

"That's what I thought he was."

"Well, to cut a long and dull story short," Hubbard said, "it was necessary for us to leave where we were. As soon as possible. Which posed certain problems. Our boat had been lost, for one thing. The weather was lousy, and we were thirty miles inside Cambodia, so we couldn't call on the conventional forces for help."

"Conventional meaning what?"

"Conventional meaning everybody but the Green Berets and us," Hubbard said. "Everybody else was forbidden to cross the Cambodian border. Well, the first chopper they sent after us got blown away, and the second one got blown away, and we were between a rock and a hard place. By the time our people worked through channels to get permission to send a conventional chopper after us, it would have been all over."

"You're not going to tell me that Art came after you?"

"Like the cavalry," Hubbard said. "He said he had

heard us on the radio and figured that unless he did something, nobody would.''

"That doesn't sound like him," Laura said. And then she felt ashamed for being disloyal.

"Well, he did it, and we were grateful," Hubbard said.

"You actually think he saved your life?"

"No question about it. Mine and Tony's and Chet Crawford's and Mac Wise's. Mac caught one a couple of weeks later."

"And that's it?" she asked. "You're doing this because he did what any man would do?"

"Any man wouldn't," Hubbard said. "What Wood did took a lot of balls. We owed him. And then he tried to collect. A couple of weeks later, he looked me up and said that he needed a package picked up at someplace along the river. So I asked him if it was drugs, and he said no, so we picked it up, and it was drugs."

"What did you do?"

"I threw it in the Mekong," Hubbard said. "And I told him what I'd done, and he said I was an ungrateful bastard, and I had to grant his point. I told him I'd square with him later, but I wasn't about to be responsible for some grunt getting himself blown away because he had stuck a needle in his arm and wasn't sure where he was, much less what he was supposed to be doing."

"And that's all of it?"

"I never saw him again over there," Hubbard said, "but somehow he found out I was in Raiford, and he sent me cigarettes, four cartons a month, as long as I was in there. No name, just a little piece of paper with 'you owe me' written on it. I guess the guards figured it was somebody who had done his time and didn't want to use his name, so they passed me the cigarettes.

"And then about eighteen months ago, he showed up in New Orleans and wanted me to pick packages out of the Gulf for him. So I told him I still owed him, but I wasn't going to be a donkey for him or anyone else. He was very upset about it. He told me that he was having a hard time making ends meet after the insurance ran out.''

"What insurance?" Laura asked.

"The insurance that was keeping you on the kidney machine," Hubbard said, and looked at her and smiled.

"He actually told you that?"

"Yeah."

"You didn't believe it?"

"No, I didn't believe it. But the son of a bitch got to me. He was very good at that. I figured he must really be over his ass in trouble to come up with a cock-and-bull story like that, so I told myself that the next thing he asked for, providing it wasn't connected with drugs, I would do. I knew he'd be back."

"And then I showed up?"

"Before you showed up, he tried to pull the same thing on Tony Pombal. Tony told him to go to hell."

"But you didn't owe me," Laura said. "So why did you offer to help me?"

"Part of it was because I talked myself into thinking that doing something for you and his kid was nearly the same thing as doing something for him."

"And the other part?"

"That was the part I talked myself out of admitting," he said. "That I would do damned near anything on the off chance that I could get in your pants."

She colored but met his eyes.

"Well, now that you have," she asked, "was it worth it?"

"I think the steaks are probably done," Hubbard said.

"You are a bastard," she said as she turned to open the broiler.

"It was so good, it scares me a little," Hubbard said.

"Scares you?"

"One way or the other," Hubbard said, "what we're up to now will be over in a couple of days. And that'll have to be the end of it."

"Because of Caroline?"

"She's as good a reason as any," Hubbard said. "There are others. But you and I have nowhere to go. You know that as well as I do."

"I suppose you're right," she said. The good feeling she had had just moments before was gone. Now she felt, she realized, even more alone than she had before she'd gone into the cabin and taken her clothes off.

"You know I'm right," he said. He got up and walked into his cabin, returning a moment later wearing a windbreaker. By then, she had laid the plate of steak and eggs on the table. He sat, wolfed the food down, and then went to the ladder to the upper deck.

"I'm going to have to see what those boats do," he said. "You might as well go back to bed."

Without waiting for a reply, he went up the ladder.

She had not, she was surprised to see, lost her appetite. She ate the steak and eggs, washed the dirty dishes, and went into the cabin. For some reason, she had a terrible urge to cry. She fought it back, took off his shirt, threw it angrily into a corner, and got into the bed, pulling the sheet over her. She would never get to sleep, she thought. She'd lay here tossing and turning for hours. Less than sixty seconds after she pulled the pillow under her head, she was fast asleep.

She woke suddenly when she felt the bed sag.

He was getting into it with her.

Now that he's explained the ground rules, like the sign she'd seen on a cabin cruiser one time, "Notice: Marriages performed by the captain are valid only during the voyage," and she knew exactly where she stood with him, a very temporary piece of ass. He was going to get what he could.

Well, to hell with you, Jack Hubbard. You've had your last piece of this ass!

He made no move to embrace her or even, she realized after a moment, to touch her. He seemed to be making an effort to occupy as little space in the bed as possible. And then he began to snore.

The bastard!

She rolled over angrily, determined to do something to him. He had been on his back, but when her rolling moved the mattress, he stirred and rolled onto his side. His arm came down on her. She tried to roll back away from him, but he pulled her against him.

He's awake. He knows exactly what he's doing!

But she realized that he wasn't awake. His breathing was regular, and the hand on her upper chest made no move toward her breast.

She moved her left hand to his hand and gently pushed it. There was no reaction. Then she moved it onto her breast. It moved now as if with a mind of its own and gently cradled her breast.

I'll bet he sleeps that way with Caroline, she thought, and then she went to sleep.

When the first light from the morning sun came through the porthole and woke Laura up, she saw that she was still under his arm, that they had slept that way. She looked over her shoulder at his face. His eyes were open, and he raised his arm to free her.

She rolled toward him, onto her back.

"This is what they call the cold, cruel light of morn," he said. "How do you feel?"

"I understand the rules," she said.

"I didn't make them."

"I know," she said.

She put her hand to his face and felt the stubble of his beard. The arm he had been holding in the air came down. His fingers on her back rolled her over onto him. She placed her face against his chest.

"Christ, that's nice," he said.

If he wants to, I'll let him.

He kissed the top of her head and then pushed himself into a sitting position.

"I wish we were someplace else," he said, and then pushed her off him and swung his feet out of bed. He went to the portholes on each side of the cabin and looked out.

"Can't see a goddamn thing," he said, and then he picked his pants off the floor and stepped into them and went through the door in the forward part of the cabin. Laura jumped out of bed and quickly put on the denim shirt and followed him.

She had never been that far forward in the *Barbara-Ann* before. The cabin there was rough and filled with equipment. She saw a ladder leading to a hatch she remembered on the foredeck. There were coils of rubber hose on hooks on one wall and tanks of oxygen and acetylene. And there was an oblong porthole close to the bow, which Hubbard had opened and through which he was looking with his binoculars.

There was a wooden crate in the center of the cabin, and Laura went to it and sat down, carefully pulling the tail of the denim shirt under her bottom to protect it from the roughly sawn lumber of the crate.

"See anything interesting?" Laura asked brightly, smiling at Hubbard, when he turned from the window and took the binoculars from his eyes.

I sound like a bubbling cheerleader, she thought.

"How could I miss it?" he asked, waving his hand at her mostly unbuttoned denim shirt. "Over there," he went on, handing her the binoculars, "I can see people moving around, but that's all I can tell they're doing. The big boat's a custom job that cost somebody a bundle. There's a twenty-foot boat on davits forward that cost at least fifteen thousand. That's an expensive dinghy. That sounds like it might be Corten's boat."

Laura focused the binoculars. There were two boats at anchor on the smoothly rolling waters off the Dry Tortugas Islands, with their bows, because of the current, pointing toward the red brick battlements of Fort Jefferson three miles away.

"I've never seen it," Laura said, trying to be serious. "I can't help you. Sorry."

"The other one is a charter boat, I think," Hubbard said. "It's an old forty-foot job, and you can see the paint flecking from here. It's the kind of boat they put out to charter. I can't see either stern board."

"Either what?" Laura asked.

"Where they paint the name on the back," he explained, looking amused.

"What do we do now?" Laura asked.

"I think we should finally get something to eat," Hubbard said. "And you better put some clothes on."

She looked at him and raised her eyebrows questioningly.

"What we are, in case anybody asks, and I think somebody will, is a small-time salvage operator and the bereaved widow who hired him to bring up her husband's body. I will call you 'Mrs. Wood,' and you will call me 'Captain Hubbard.' Bereaved widows in those circumstances do not go around in the hired hand's shirt with their tail hanging out."

She stuck her tongue out at him, and they smiled at each other.

"What do you mean, you think somebody will ask?" Laura inquired.

"Those boats are not out there by coincidence," Hubbard explained. "You can bet they'll take as close a look at us as they can." He pushed himself off the gas hoses and walked out of the cabin and down the passageway.

Laura, when she got to the cabin, found him there, strapping the holstered snubnosed .38 revolver onto his belt in the small of his back. Then he put on a loose-fitting, faded, and grease-soiled safari jacket. She saw that even if you knew it was there, the .38 was just about invisible under the jacket.

She modestly waited for him to leave the cabin before she started to change, and then she wondered why.

I've already let him know that I am shameless, lewd, and lascivious.

She went to her luggage and took out underwear and a pair of slacks and a blouse. She took off the blue denim shirt and hung it on a hanger in the closet, and then she gave in to an impulse. She went naked to the cabin door and opened it a crack. Hubbard was on his knees, taking bacon and eggs from the refrigerator. Laura opened the door wide.

"Oh, Captain!" Laura called sweetly. "Yoo hoo, Captain!"

When Hubbard looked at her, she put her hands behind her head and threw him a stripteaser's bump.

He laughed out loud.

"What did you say you did before you got married?"

"I was a sweet and innocent college girl," she said. "Couldn't you guess?"

She closed the door and got dressed. Then she thought about what he had said and dressed for the part of a bereaved widow. She parted her hair in the middle and arranged it tightly in a bun at her neck. Then she took sunglasses from her purse and put them on. Finally, she made the bed and arranged the cabin so that in case anyone looked into it, there would be no evidence that two people were sharing bed and cabin.

When she went into the cabin, it was heavy with the pleasant smell of frying bacon and brewing coffee.

"There's a coffee table," Hubbard said, pointing to the rear of the cabin, "and on the other side of the door, folding chairs. Set them up on the aft deck; let's give them something to look at."

After she had set the table up and then laid it with tableware, and as she was carrying their two plates of bacon and eggs in one hand and the coffeepot in the other, she saw him fussing with the curtain at the aft cabin, where the coffee table and chairs had been. He was working the actions of the Army rifle and the pump shotgun and putting them vertically on racks built for them beneath the curtain.

She was startled by the sound of a radio being tuned

right above her head. She looked up, saw a weatherproof speaker mounted high on the cabin bulkhead, just under an eave.

"All the comforts of home," Laura said when he came out and sat down.

"With what we have to charge you for our services, Mrs. Wood," Hubbard said, "we try to provide every comfort."

"I have no complaints at all, Captain Hubbard," she said.

Hubbard had just poured a second cup of coffee when he said softly, "They're putting the big boat in the water."

"Can I look?" she asked.

"That would be the natural thing to do," Hubbard said. He got up and went into the cabin. "I'm going to get the binoculars."

Laura turned around and looked at the larger boat. There were two men on the deck over the cabin doing something to a white boat that was mounted there and two more men on the deck that ran alongside the cabin. As she watched, a davit picked the white boat and swung it over the side and began to lower it. When it was level with the deck, the two men stabilized it and she saw and thought she faintly heard one of them open his mouth and call something. A man came out of a door in the cabin wall and climbed into the white boat, which was then lowered the rest of the way into the water.

She wished she could see better and turned to see where Hubbard was with the binoculars. He was leaning on the cabin door, watching what was going on through the binoculars. He was not about to turn them over to her, and so she turned again and watched. The man in the boat unhooked the cables on which the boat had been lowered into the water and then stood at the control console.

She could hear the sound of the engine's starter, but it was a long time before the engine caught. A cloud of blue smoke came out of the exhausts and floated across the water. Then the sound of the engine changed pitch, and the boat turned away from the yacht. The bow came quickly out of the water.

She felt gentle fingers on her shoulder and turned to see Hubbard extending the binoculars to her.

"Recognize that man?" he asked.

She put the binoculars to her eyes and had trouble finding the boat and then focusing the binoculars when she did. But then everything was clear.

"That's Dexter Corten," she said.

He snatched the binoculars out of her hand and stared intently through them.

CHAPTER

13

"You do the talking," Hubbard said. "Remember that you're the one who hired me and that I'm just your hired hand."

"What am I supposed to say?"

"Just play it by ear," Hubbard told her. "He wants to talk to you. Let's hear what he has to say."

He dropped to his knees and took several lengths of line, a boat hook, and two woven rope bumpers from cabinets mounted against the cabin wall. He hung the rope bumpers over the side and then stood with the boat hook in one hand and the lengths of line in the other as the big boat approached.

The boat, a twenty-one-foot inboard center console fisherman, came off the plane, approached the *Barbara-Ann*, and then went into reverse until it had stopped.

"Captain," Dexter Corten called to Hubbard, "do you have a Mrs. Laura Wood aboard?"

Dexter Corten was a lithe, suntanned man in his late thirties. He wore sunglasses that hid his eyes. He was wearing an expensive knit shirt and a faded pair of blue jeans, and his feet were in rubber-soled leather running shoes.

Laura stepped beside Hubbard so that Corten could see her.

"May I come aboard?" Corten asked.

Hubbard looked at Laura as if for permission. Laura nodded. Hubbard tossed the two coils of line into the *Shamrock* and then reached down and caught the *Shamrock*'s stainless-steel railing with the boat hook. Corten turned the engine off and then tied the line to a cleat on the *Shamrock*'s bow and threw the loose end of the line to Hubbard, who made it fast.

"I think one line'll hold her," Corten said.

"It's your boat, sir," Hubbard said, catching the unused coil of line. Corten stepped from the *Shamrock* onto the *Barbara-Ann*'s swim platform and then climbed up the ladder into the cabin.

"Mrs. Wood," he said, going to Laura and offering her his hand. "Mrs. Wood," he repeated when he had caught both of her hands in his, "I'm so terribly sorry, ashamed, about everything."

"Ashamed?" Laura asked, surprised.

"The truth of the matter is that I am ashamed of myself," he said. "What the Episcopal church calls a sin of omission." Then he turned to Hubbard. "My name is Dexter Corten," he said. "I understand you tried to see me yesterday."

"That's right," Hubbard said, taking the extended hand. Hubbard had the tangential thought that the business about miserable people having clammy handshakes was so much crap. He instinctively disliked Dexter Corten, whose grip was firm and warm.

"A pleasure, Captain," Corten said, and turned to Laura. "I hope you can understand, Mrs. Wood," Corten said, "my state of mind after the accident. The truth of the matter is that I just lost control of myself."

"I don't quite understand," Laura said.

"One moment, we were all having a good time," Corten said. "Everybody standing on the deck of the *Non-Deductible* having a drink and watching Art's plane come in for a landing. And the next moment, without warning, it happened."

"The crash, you mean?" Hubbard asked innocently.

Corten nodded his head. "Art's plane crashed," he said. "I hope you can believe, Mrs. Wood, that there was nothing anyone on the *Non-Deductible* could do. For whatever comfort it might give, he didn't suffer. It was over in a moment."

Laura said nothing.

"The bottom line is that after we called the Coast Guard, I just went to pieces. I seemed to be incapable of thought, of recognizing my obligations, much less doing anything about them," Corten said.

"I don't quite follow you," Laura said.

"What I should have done, obviously, is immediately gotten in touch with you, not only to express my sympathy but to tell you that I would take care of everything that had to be done. About getting Art's body up, I mean. I'm truly sorry I can't think of a more delicate way to put that."

"I've hired Captain Hubbard to recover my husband's body," Laura said.

"Yes," Corten said. "So I understand. That's one of the reasons I'm here, to talk about that."

"What is there to talk about?" Laura asked.

"As my associate, Mr. Frazier, told Captain Hubbard this afternoon, I'm going to assume whatever costs are involved," Corten said. "I was led to believe that Captain Hubbard told Mr. Frazier he was going to tell you that."

"That's very kind of you," Laura said.

"And did he tell you?"

Laura looked to Hubbard for guidance. Hubbard, barely perceptibly, nodded his head.

"Yes, he did," Laura said.

"As I see it," Corten said, "Art was working for me when the accident happened. Perhaps not technically, not legally, but morally. I've always felt responsible for people who work for me. Now, nothing's going to bring Art back unfortunately, but doing whatever I can to make things as right as I can is the least I can do. I should have gotten in touch with you immediately to tell you that. Before you got in touch with this man, with Captain Hubbard."

"I don't understand," Laura said. "What difference does it make who . . ."—she hesitated—"brings Art's body up?"

"I've already made other arrangements," Corten said. "When I began to understand what my obligations were, I made arrangements to hire the best salvage people I could find. No reflection at all, Captain. I'm sure that you're perfectly qualified to do this sort of thing, but I was told that the best people around are Key West Salvors. Are you familiar with them?"

"I know who they are," Hubbard said.

"They're supposed to be the best equipped for this sort of operation," Corten said. "And they assure me that they will put out for here first thing in the morning, just as soon as they can get their hands on the charts the Coast Guard made when they were out here."

"I see," Hubbard said. "But all we have to do is bring up Mr. Wood's body and an identifiable piece of the airplane. This isn't really that big a salvage operation."

"Let me make it clear, Captain, that I intend to see you adequately compensated for what you have done so far. You just come up with a figure for your expenses plus whatever else you feel you're entitled to, and I'll give you a check. I stand behind everything Mr. Frazier told you yesterday."

"Why don't you just pay me for doing what Mrs. Wood has hired me to do?"

"I was afraid you'd take that attitude, frankly," Corten said.

"What do you mean by that?" Hubbard snapped.

"Mrs. Wood," Corten said. "What do you really know about this man?"

"My husband knew him in the service," Laura said. "What am I supposed to know about him?"

"The last thing in the world I want for you is more grief," Corten said. "Let me put it to you this way, Captain Hubbard. Would you consider yourself adequately compensated for your services if I paid you your expenses and five thousand dollars besides?"

"Why would you want to do that?" Hubbard asked.

"That's really none of your concern, is it?" Corten said. "But I'll spell it out for you. You have an unsavory reputation, Hubbard. The Coast Guard knows all about you. I don't want you preying on Mrs. Wood."

"Mrs. Wood has signed a contract with me," Hubbard said, "under which I will be paid only if and when I recover her husband's body and an identifiable part of the airplane. How is that preying on her? I resent that."

"I'd hoped that this could be settled amicably," Corten said. "But if you insist, Hubbard." He turned to Laura. "Let me assure you of this, Mrs. Wood. You don't have to worry about paying this man a thin dime. By tomorrow afternoon, Key West Salvors will be here with the equipment and the men and the expertise to do what has to be done. And with one more thing, a license from the State of Florida to conduct a marine salvage operation. Did *Captain* Hubbard tell you that a license is required? And that he doesn't have one? And that he can't get one because he's a convicted felon?"

Laura stole a look at Hubbard over Corten's shoulder. He shook his head no.

"No, he didn't," Laura said.

"Did you know that he was a convicted felon?" Corten went on. Again Hubbard cued Laura to say no by shaking his head.

"All I know is that he and my husband were friends in the service," she said.

"*Captain* Hubbard," Corten said, "wasn't exactly forthcoming about that. He told Mr. Frazier that someone had recommended him to you."

"What difference does it make?" Laura asked.

"Not to speak ill of the dead," Corten said, "but you know as well as I do that Art was often too trusting a man. Some of the people he thought of as his friends weren't really friends. You know that, Mrs. Wood."

She nodded her agreement.

"I really dislike bargaining with people like you," Corten said to Hubbard. "But I'm going to make you one final offer. I want you to think it over very carefully, to consider your own best interests. I won't waste my time appealing to your sense of right and wrong. But I want you to remember that if you don't find the body, you don't get a dime. And you really don't have much of chance of finding it without the Coast Guard charts. So this is the choice you have to make. You can stick around and watch Key West Salvors do what you're simply incapable of doing and not get a dime, or you can take my check for ten thousand dollars right now."

Hubbard glanced at Laura Woods and was disappointed but not, he thought, really surprised to see doubt in her eyes. It all gets down to the dollar sign, he thought. The smart thing for him to do was to take the ten thousand and go home.

"What's in that airplane, anyway?" Hubbard asked. "Beside Arthur Wood's body, I mean?"

"What the hell do you mean by that?" Dexter Corten asked angrily.

"I'm a lousy judge of human nature," Laura Wood said softly. "But I know enough about people like you, Mr. Corten, to know that whenever they start giving things away out of the goodness of their heart, to do the right thing, you have something they want."

"I don't deserve that," Dexter Corten said. "That's unfair!"

"That's the way I feel," Laura said.

"Then you're a fool, Mrs. Wood," Corten said. He turned to face Hubbard. "You heard my offer," he said. "And nothing I heard about you suggests that you're a fool. What's it to be?"

"I'm going to recover Arthur Wood's body," Hubbard said. "And anybody who gets in my way is going to get hurt."

Without a word, Dexter Corten climbed down the ladder from the cockpit to the swim platform, stepped into the *Shamrock*, and went to the controls. He turned the key, and the starter ground and then died. The engine would not start.

Hubbard stepped to the railing. Corten looked up at him.

"My battery is dead," Corten said.

Hubbard untied the line to the *Shamrock* and let it fall in the water, and then he took the boat hook and pushed the *Shamrock* away from the *Barbara-Ann*.

"You miserable son of a bitch!" Corten shouted. He opened a compartment on the *Shamrock*'s console and picked up a microphone and spoke into it. There was not, he realized in a moment, enough battery power left to operate the short-wave radio. The *Shamrock*, caught by the current, drifted away from the *Barbara-Ann*.

Corten tried one more time to start the engine with his dead battery, and then he began to frantically wave his arms to catch the attention of somebody on the *Non-Deductible*. It was a long time before he caught anyone's attention, and then it took more time before they could weigh the *Non-Deductible*'s anchor and get her under way and then maneuver the large yacht close enough to get a line aboard the *Shamrock*.

Two men came into the cockpit of the other boat. Hubbard examined them carefully through the binoculars and then handed the binoculars to Laura.

"The one with the red face is Fallon," he said.

Laura, by now able to cope with the binoculars,

quickly picked out a man matching Hubbard's description. He was smiling. She shifted the glasses. The other man was wearing a broad grin at Corten's plight, and as she watched, he turned and called to someone inside the cabin.

"I've seen him before," Laura said to Hubbard.

"Who? Fallon?"

"If that's his name," she said. "The man with the red face."

"Where'd you see him?"

"At the airport once or twice."

"With your husband?" Hubbard asked.

"Yes."

"I wonder what they had to talk about," Hubbard said.

"Jack," Laura asked, "why did you do that to him?"

"To Corten, you mean?"

"Yes. I mean, really, that was nasty."

"Angry people make mistakes," Hubbard said. "And I got the feeling that nothing would make Mr. Corten angrier than being made a fool of."

The remark was sobering, and her smile vanished.

"*We* may have made a mistake," Laura said. "That was one of those offers you're not supposed to refuse."

"You noticed that, did you?" Hubbard chuckled. "Well, not to worry. Here comes the cavalry."

She followed his glance. Several miles to the east, there was a battered and rusty work boat slowly plodding through the sea.

"Pombal?" Laura asked. Hubbard nodded.

The workboat, which Laura thought looked slightly less seaworthy than Humphrey Bogart's *African Queen*, took a long time to cross the gently rolling seas to them, but eventually it was a hundred yards off the stern of the *Barbara-Ann*. The sound of the diesel engine died. Tony Pombal appeared on the bow, effortlessly picked up a six-foot anchor that Laura knew must weigh well over a hundred pounds, and tossed it into the water. Then he set it by jerking on its heavy line and tied it to a stanchion. Pombal then went to a square-ended aluminum dinghy carried crosswise on the deck and shoved it into the water. He pulled it back to the work boat by its line, stepped in, and jerked a one-cylinder outboat into life. A man came out of the wheelhouse, stepped into the dinghy, and sat down.

"I'll be damned," Hubbard said. The second man on the work boat was the wiry little man Laura had last seen waving goodbye to them in Biloxi, Chet Crawford.

The dinghy, the one-lunger outboard roaring like a furious wasp, made its way to the *Barbara-Ann*. In a moment, Tony Pombal and Chet Crawford were standing on the aft deck.

"Why, Chester," Hubbard said wryly, "how nice to see you!"

"Shit," Chet Crawford said.

"I figured we'd likely need him," Pombal said. "So I told him to get his ass on a plane."

"But Chester was busy," Hubbard said.

"He owed Wood as much as you and me," Pombal said. "And I heard something very interesting."

"What was that?"

"Wood was carrying something worth a lot of money out here," Pombal said.

"Laura says not," Hubbard said. Pombal's eyebrows went up at Hubbard's use of Laura's first name.

"I vacuumed that airplane just before he took off," Laura insisted. "There wasn't anything on it but Mr. Corten's attaché case."

"Oh," Hubbard said. "That's the first you mentioned Corten's attaché case."

"Art did that for him all the time," Laura said. "Carried paperwork back and forth to the *Non-Deductible*."

"Paperwork," Hubbard said.

"I didn't think anything about it, Jack," Laura said. "I'm sorry."

"Well, let's say that if Corten is very anxious to get his paperwork back, that explains a lot," Hubbard said.

"I tried to call in some favors with the Coast Guard," Pombal said. "But I got nowhere with getting the chart. I did find out that Key West Salvors asked for it. As soon as they produce the salvage license, Jack, the Coast Guard is going to give it to them."

"So I heard," Hubbard said.

"How are we going to find the goddamn plane without a chart?" Crawford asked.

"Mrs. Wood," Hubbard said, "has had a copy all along."

"Well, give me a beer and we'll have a look at it," Pombal said.

"A couple of guys tried to knife me in Fort Myers," Hubbard said. "And then Corten, that's the big boat, came over here and offered me ten thousand dollars to go home."

Pombal nodded.

"Who's on the head boat?" Pombal asked, nodding his head toward it.

"A man named Fallon," Hubbard said. "He came to the boat in Fort Myers and offered me thirty thousand if I could bring up something from the airplane that would prove that Art Wood was doing something illegal. So they could get out of paying off on the insurance."

"Paperwork, my ass!" Chet Crawford said.

"What do you mean, we, white man?" Pombal said. Hubbard and Crawford looked at him and then burst into laughter.

After a moment, Laura's curiosity got the better of her.

"What's so funny?"

Hubbard looked at her. His eyes were smiling. "Did you ever hear about the time, Laura," he asked, "when the Lone Ranger and Tonto were riding across the desert, and suddenly they were surrounded by hundreds of howling Indians. So the Lone Ranger turns to Tonto and says, 'What are we going to do, faithful Indian companion?' And Tonto looks at him and says . . .''

"What do you mean, we, white man?" Laura finished for him.

He nodded and chuckled, and then Pombal and Crawford started to laugh again, and Hubbard joined in. It was probably nervous laughter, Laura thought, but it was laughter. In some perverse way, they liked their situation. It was some kind of a challenge.

Crawford immediately proved his point.

"What the hell are we laughing about?" he asked.

"I don't know about me, little man," Tony Pombal said, "but I know you're crazy."

"What are we going to do, Skipper?" Chet Crawford asked seriously.

"I think the tactical situation," Hubbard said, mockingly military, "calls for a diversion operation."

"Like what?"

"Let's shake the bastards up a little," Hubbard said. "Let's find the airplane, and mark it with a balloon."

"How the hell are you going to do that?" Crawford asked.

"After Laura gets the chart and we stand on the upper deck and point and gesture and act like we know just what we're doing, I'm going to get suited up and go over the side and go down to the bottom. After swimming around for a while, I'll tie the balloon line to a rock."

Pombal looked thoughtful. "Meanwhile, Crawford goes back to the boat, and is busy rigging the derrick and checking the auxiliary engine."

"And what are you going to be doing while I'm doing all this work?" Crawford demanded.

"I'm going to suit up and go over the side with Jack," Pombal said. "And then I'm going to come right back aboard and watch everybody."

Hubbard nodded. "Get the chart, Laura, and then go on the upper deck with Crawford."

CHAPTER
14

"Jesus Christ," Chet Crawford said when Hubbard and Pombal came onto the deck in wet suits with diving gear. "Talk about pack rats. How the hell old is that stuff, anyway?"

"Jackass," Pombal said, "we want to give them bubbles to look at. You have the imagination of a sea turtle."

Pombal and Hubbard, Laura saw, were enjoying themselves. She didn't understand the business about the bubbles, though, and asked about it.

Crawford looked at her in annoyance, making it clear that he thought she was an intruder.

"Some of this equipment," Hubbard explained as he put the tanks onto his back, "permits the oxygen-exhausted gas to escape. That makes bubbles. The newer, better equipment recycles the exhaust gas, and there's nothing to bubble. So we're going to use this to keep their interest high."

"But won't they see there's only one set of bubbles?"

"I'm going to tow Tony's tanks around on a length

of line," Hubbard said, delighted with himself. "Jack Hubbard and Company, masters of deception!"

"I wonder what that silly man is doing, the man with shark gun will wonder," Crawford said. "Just before he lets you have the spear in the ass."

"Get in the goddamn boat and go back to the work boat," Pombal said.

"Try to look like you know what you're doing," Hubbard said. "Get your hands dirty."

"Jesus Christ, I don't know why I let the goddamn Portugee talk me into this," Crawford said. But he handed Laura the chart and went down to the cockpit and then down the ladder to the swim platform and into the dinghy. The engine coughed and started, and in a moment Laura could see him in the stern of the dinghy, heading across the water to the work boat.

Hubbard and Pombal went down the ladder to the cockpit and stood there a moment, checking each other's equipment. Laura saw that Hubbard had three devices snapped to his belt. They were about the diameter of a can of soup but twice as long. They were neatly wrapped with line, and she understood that these were the balloons he had been talking about. She saw a diver's knife and other diving equipment she didn't understand, and then she saw something that disturbed her. Hubbard had tied the dagger with which the men on the dock at Fort Myers had tried to kill him to his upper left arm. There was a length of line tied to the hilt of the knife in such a manner that the line that held it to his arm in a series of slip knots would, if the knife came loose or was taken, keep him from losing it. The way he had it tied to his upper arm, the hilt of the knife extended below his elbow. She would have thought he would tie it right side up, and then she realized that this was obviously not the first time he'd tied that kind of a knife to his arm. He had it tied on right.

"He's almost there," Hubbard said. "You want to go?"

Pombal nodded and pulled his goggles and mouthpiece into place. Laura felt Hubbard's hand run across her back and then squeeze her upper arm. She turned to look at him. In that moment, ready for the water, he stepped onto the railing and over the side. A moment later, Tony Pombal followed him.

She looked over at the work boat. Chet Crawford was hauling the dinghy aboard. She looked back at the water close to the boat. She saw bubbles coming to the surface.

She wanted to look at the other boats and told herself that she shouldn't. Then she realized that that didn't make any sense. It was perfectly natural for her to be curious, and so she looked. Men on both boats were looking in their direction through binoculars.

She had a sudden, nearly overpowering urge to go to the toilet, and so she went quickly into the cabin. She'd done that as long as she could remember. Every time she got excited, she had to go.

When she came out of the master's cabin, Tony Pombal, naked from the waist down, was standing in the center of the cabin, grunting as he pulled the top of the wet suit off. She was startled. There had been no sensation of movement as he came aboard. She realized that what she had expected was that his head would appear by the side of the boat, in which case she would have been asked to help him climb aboard.

He got the wet suit jacket mostly off, and she saw a two-foot, angry red scar on his right side. Somewhere, sometime Tony Pombal had been deeply and badly cut.

She went into the cabin. "Don't turn around, here's your pants," she said, picking them off the deck and handing them to him. "You want a towel?"

"Please," he said, looking over his shoulder at her.

She went into the head, got him a towel, and laid it on his shoulder.

He dried his legs and put his underpants and pants on and then turned to her.

"I didn't hear, or feel, you come back on," she said.

"You weren't supposed to," he said. "Does Jack still keep that M1A of his behind the curtains? Or don't you know?"

"On the left-hand side," she said.

He pulled a knit shirt over his head and then took the rifle from its rack. He removed the magazine, unloaded it, reloaded it, and put it back into the rifle. He worked the action, loading a cartridge into the chamber, and then put the rifle back into the rack.

"I think it would be a good idea if you went up on deck and kept an eye on the water and the other boats," Pombal told her.

"Oh, my God," Laura said. "I didn't think."

"If they put somebody in the water," Pombal said, "they'll wait until they see where Jack's going."

Laura quickly climbed the ladder to the upper deck and put the binoculars to her eyes. She looked first at the other boats, where men were studying the surface of the water through binoculars. Then she searched the surface of the water until she saw the disturbance caused by the escaping bubbles. There were two distinct areas of disturbance. She wondered how, since no one was taking air from the tanks Jack Hubbard was towing behind him, he was causing them to bubble. The answer to that question, she thought, is that he knows what he's doing. It was a comfortable thought.

She looked at the work boat. Crawford had erected a derrick on the deck. A fifty-five-gallon barrel was hanging from its cable. As Laura watched, it very slowly descended to the surface of the water and disappeared.

"They'll wonder about that," Pombal said, chuckling. She saw that he was standing immediately under the hatch to the upper deck.

"What's he doing?"

"That's what they're going to be asking each other," Pombal replied.

"What's in the barrel?"

"Iron bars," Pombal replied. Then he startled her by

asking bluntly: "What have you got going with Jack?"

"I never saw Jack Hubbard," Laura replied, "until I went to New Orleans."

"I saw the way he looked at you," Pombal said. "You've had plenty of time to work on him since then."

She looked down the hatch directly at him but didn't say anything.

"Jack is very unlucky with women," Pombal said. "That's none of my business. What is my business is whether we're in this because Jack still figures he owes your husband for saving our ass or whether he's doing it for you."

"What's the difference?"

"Lady, Tony Pombal don't owe you a thing," he said.

"Then I guess when Jack comes up," Laura replied, "you better tell him you're leaving."

"Jesus!" he said. Then: "Well, I asked, and you told me."

"Tell me about Caroline," Laura said.

"That's none of your business, is it?"

"I don't know," Laura said. "I thought you were asking if I'd gone to bed with him. The answer is yes. But I don't know what that meant to him."

"Well, you got to him," Pombal said after a moment. "Angy saw it back at Port Boca Grande. I saw it just now."

"And where does Caroline fit in?"

"Did Jack tell you he'd done time?" Pombal asked.

"Yes."

"He tell you why?"

"Yes."

"He tell you she took everything he owned?" Pombal asked.

"No."

"When he got out of prison, he needed a job, right then. And Jack doesn't ask anybody for help. I didn't know he was out of jail until six months after. So what he did was get a shitty job working on rigs in the Gulf. Underwater maintenance work. Any jackass with an air tank can do it, and Jack's one of the best divers in the business. So he was out on a rig for a couple of weeks, and then he went to New Orleans.''

"Why?''

"He'd been in jail for a long time,'' Pombal said. He waited until Laura understood his meaning.

"And that's how he met her?'' Laura asked.

Pombal nodded. "She was working the bar at Caroline's. Only it wasn't Caroline's then. It was called Peter's. And a couple of guys, tourists, were giving her a hard time, and Jack had a load on, and he played Sir Galahad. He has a tendency to do that. You know what I mean?''

"I think so.'' As he is now, Laura thought.

"So the way things are in the French Quarter is that when tourists get involved with guys off oil rigs, the guy from the oil rig is wrong. So they take Jack off to the slammer, and the judge fines him about six hundred dollars, which is about four hundred more than he has, or work the time off in the Orleans Parish jail.

"But Caroline hears about this, and she goes and pays the fine and gets him out of jail. Now, Jack doesn't like to be in anybody's debt, much less a French Quarter hooker's, but he's not that much of a fool. So he tells her he'll pay her back and lets her get him out of the can.''

"And he paid her back, and that was the start of their touching friendship?''

"There's more. Jack goes back out on the rig, and they find out that J. Hubbard, diving bum, is really Jack Hubbard, ex-Navy chief warrant officer, one of the guys who's done some really deep sea diving. You know what gas saturation means?''

"No.''

"It's not important,'' he said. "But Jack has dived just about as deep as anybody ever has, and he understands the technology. He's not just a strong set of lungs. Anyway, the next thing you know, he's over in the North Sea, where one of their rigs got knocked over. You must have seen it in the papers. Eleven people trapped inside?''

"Yes, I think so," Laura said.

"So Jack gases himself up—"

"Excuse me?"

"Saturates his body with gas so he can stay down there a long time," Pombal explained, "and he goes down there. Alone. A hundred and ninety feet. And he cuts the rig apart with C-4." He looked at her and saw incomprehension. "C-4 is an explosive," he explained. "What he did was cut the compartments where the people were trapped away from the rest of the rig with explosives."

"I understand," Laura said.

"He was down there about four hours more than he was supposed to be," Pombal said. "And what was supposed to happen next was that the derricks on the surface would then pull the people up. But when Jack was decompressing and they had it halfway up, one of the cables snapped. So there's this thing hanging on one cable that's about to break. So Jack goes back down because there's nobody else there who knows how to, and he hooks up another cable, and he rigs more air tanks."

"You're telling me he's a hero?"

"I'm telling you where Caroline got the money to buy the bar," Pombal said.

"I don't understand."

"They laid a lot of money on him," Pombal said. "Right at seventy-five thousand. And flew him back to the States on one of those little private jets. So he goes to the Royal Orleans and takes a suite and lays a hundred-dollar bill on a bellboy and tells him there's another one for him just as soon as he delivers a red-headed hooker named Caroline to the suite."

Pombal stopped when he saw the expression on Laura's face.

"What he's going to do, you see," he explained, "is give her her four hundred back with enough interest so that he doesn't owe her any more. She's a hooker, you understand what I'm saying to you? Men like Jack can't stand owing a hooker."

"I understand," Laura said.

"So what happens is that Caroline gets there, and what she finds is Jack just about dead from helium saturation decompression."

"I don't know what that means," Laura said.

"After you deep dive, you decompress in a tank. Sometimes it doesn't work. Jack had done what he was supposed to do; he was in the decompression tank thirty hours, but it didn't work. Somebody said that what might have given him trouble was coming back to the States on the jet right away, that maybe the oxygen in the airplane is what caused it. Nobody knows for sure. All anybody knows for sure is that if Caroline hadn't got him over to the Tulane Medical School Hospital when she did, he would be dead. He damn near died in their decompression tank. He was paralyzed for three weeks, and every day Caroline came to see him."

"The whore with the heart of gold," Laura said.

Pombal bit off whatever reply he was going to make to that and instead said: "So now he really owed her, you understand? He just couldn't give her money and get out of it."

"I see," Laura said softly.

"So most of the seventy-five thousand went to buy her the bar. I think he owns forty-nine percent of it. There's a corporation."

"He didn't want to owe a hooker, so he winds up owning half a whorehouse," Laura said.

"That's what Angy said, too," Pombal said. "But it's not that way. For one thing, it's not a whorehouse."

"It's not?" Laura asked sarcastically.

"No. It's a place where working girls can meet people," Pombal explained. "That's all. You order a drink in there, you get a drink, not iced tea."

Laura looked at him in surprise, remembering the straight glass of scotch she had been served.

"And there's no pimps and no drugs, and nobody gets rolled," Pombal said.

"And Caroline is really nothing more than a house mother at a sorority, right?" Laura said sarcastically.

"You asked, I told you," Pombal said.

"I'm surprised he hasn't married her," Laura said, "since they owe each other so much."

"I don't think Jack will ever get married again," Pombal said. "He was badly burned, really badly burned, when he was. And if he ever did, he wouldn't marry an ex-hooker."

"Of course not," Laura said sarcastically. "What would people think?"

Pombal gave her a dirty look. "I'm going to get a beer," he said, and disappeared from view.

A moment later, she wondered if Pombal had intended to tell her something. He had said that Jack wouldn't marry an ex-hooker. She wasn't an ex-hooker. It wasn't much to pin any hopes on, but on the other hand, Pombal had talked to her, and if he didn't approve of her, he wouldn't have talked to her.

And I'm a widow, Laura thought, and not an ex-hooker.

When Hubbard went in the water, he swam straight to the bottom. He wanted to know how far down the bottom was, what the bottom was like, and what the visibility would be, and he wanted to take a couple of handfuls of sand and see what the currents were like.

When he reached the bottom, he could look up and see the surface and the hull of the *Barbara-Ann*, but he could see very little around him. It was much darker than he had expected, and he could see no more than fifteen or twenty feet. That might, he knew, have something to do with the angle at which the rays of the sun were striking the surface of the water, reflecting the light away rather than permitting it to penetrate. Or the poor visibility might have something to do with particles of algae or sand or something suspended in the water, which would also turn away the sun's light.

When he scooped handfuls of sand from the bottom and let them filter through his fingers, that served only to decrease the visibility further; he could tell nothing about the currents. He guessed that at the moment, the current was negligible.

He pushed himself ten feet off the bottom and then began to swim slowly. He planned to stay down at least thirty minutes, perhaps as long as an hour or forty-five minutes. Since he had no destination in mind, there was no sense expending more energy than was required to keep the people on Fallon's boat and on Corten's *Non-Deductible* guessing what the hell he was up to.

Wet suit divers who make a lot of frantic motion attract sharks. Hubbard was armed against sharks with an air gun and three spare spears and chargers, but he considered the gun useless. He was very much afraid of sharks. He had once recovered the body of a man whose buttocks and upper leg had been bitten by sharks. The massive muscles had been neatly severed and the chunks of flesh torn off by jaws of incredible strength.

He swam slowly, using only his legs. One hand held the tanks that were supposed to convince the watchers that Pombal was down here with him. The other hand, flat against his side, held the alumimum-frame air gun.

Five minutes from the moment he had entered the water, when he was swimming on a course that would put him off the sterns of both the other boats, a dull, silvery reflection caught his eye. It was the sort of reflection that could be made by the undulation of a shark's underbelly as the shark moved through the water.

He stopped kicking and carefully turned his head to where he had seen the silvery flicker of light. There was nothing at his depth or above him. But then he saw the light again and swam toward it. It was not moving. After a moment, he saw what it was. It was the float of a seaplane.

He swam very slowly toward it. It was entirely possible that if the windows had been broken or the door was open, a shark would be leisurely eating the body inside. If there had been a school of sharks that had found the body as little as twenty minutes ago, there would be nothing left of the body.

The plane was on its back, probably turned as it sank by the buoyancy of the floats, which had not been enough to bring the plane to the surface but had been enough to turn it over. There was no shark or for that matter any fish. The body of the pilot was still strapped to the seat. Twenty or more crabs were feeding on it.

Hubbard averted his eyes, forced the image from his mind, and swam to the tail of the airplane. The compass on his wrist told him that the nose tail axis of the plane was very nearly East-West. He swam directly away from the tail, using his arms and his legs steadily. He carefully counted two hundred and fifty strokes, and he estimated his position as that many yards or perhaps fifty yards more.

He stopped swimming, pulled his arms against his sides, and began to sink to the bottom. As he sank, his body moved into an erect position. When he reached the bottom, he sank into a squatting position and looked around for a rock. He had trouble finding one. The bottom was sandy, and there was vegetation. All he managed to do was stir up sand. Then he found something encrusted with barnacles, an object ten inches around. It could easily be a beer can tossed over board two years before.

Whatever it was, once he buried it in the sand, it would be enough to anchor the balloon.

Tying the line to the barnacle-encrusted object and then burying it in the sand took him five minutes. Then he activated the gas bottle, and the balloon filled and rose to the surface. Hubbard sat on the bottom of the Gulf for another five minutes to make sure that wave action and the wind on the surface would not dislodge the balloon's anchor. Then he suddenly pushed himself erect, looked at his compass, and started to swim back toward the *Barbara-Ann*.

CHAPTER
15

When Jack Hubbard came out of the shower, Laura was waiting for him, holding out a towel.

"Whatever," Hubbard said, "will Pombal think?"

"I don't give a damn what he thinks," Laura replied. "And he knew that we'd been to bed before I came in here."

"You told him, no doubt?"

"I confirmed what he suspected," Laura said.

Hubbard finished drying himself and then pulled on a pair of khaki pants. He walked into the cabin.

"No action on either boat," Pombal said.

"The plane is two hundred fifty, maybe three hundred yards due west of the marker," Hubbard said.

"You found it?" Pombal asked, surprised.

"Dumb luck," Hubbard said.

"Is Art in it?" Laura asked.

Hubbard met her eyes and nodded his head.

Laura sensed Pombal's eyes on her and looked at him.

"I'm sorry that he's dead, of course," she said. "But I'm not going to fake tears I don't feel."

Pombal nodded his head.

"He didn't crash on landing," Hubbard said. Pombal jerked his head to look at him. "Somebody rigged a bomb."

"How do you know?" Pombal asked.

"The instrument panel was gone," Hubbard said. "I don't know, but what I guess is that somebody who knows about airplanes wired it into the low-altitude warning buzzer."

"You're saying somebody killed my husband?" Laura asked in shocked disbelief. "With a bomb?"

"A couple of sticks of dynamite, probably," Hubbard said. "Instead of wiring them to the ignition switch, they wired them to the low-altitude warning buzzer circuit."

"Wouldn't that blow it in the air?" Pombal said. "The people on Corten's boat would have seen that."

"We don't know that they didn't," Hubbard said. "But if I were going to do it, I'd wire a two-stage detonator. When the low-altitude warning circuit went off, it would activate a trembler switch. Then as soon as there was the shock of the floats hitting the water, it would blow."

"Yeah," Pombal said after thinking it over a moment. "And you wouldn't have to know a hell of a lot about detonators, either, would you?"

"And to give Corten a fair shake," Hubbard went on, "if you weren't thinking about explosives, you would think the explosion was the gas tanks."

"Somebody didn't want him to bring Corten's attaché case out here," Pombal said. "Jesus, Skipper, what the hell's going on?"

"Well, there's an attaché case in the plane," Hubbard said.

"Why didn't you bring it up?"

"Because there's three of us and about seven of

them," Hubbard said, "and I didn't know what had happened while I was down there."

"There's four of us," Laura said.

"Yeah, sure," Hubbard said, and smiled at her. "Four."

Laura looked over his shoulder.

"Oh, my God," she said. "Look!"

They looked. There was a fire on the work boat. A dense cloud of black smoke was rising into the air.

Hubbard and Pombal looked at each other.

"What do they expect us to do?" Hubbard asked rhetorically.

"Go over there in this," Pombal said. "You got an inflatable?"

"Who stays here?"

"One of us better," Pombal said. "And that's my boat. You stay."

Hubbard nodded, and then they went to work wordlessly. He motioned for Pombal to follow him. They went through the master's cabin to the forward cabin and came back a moment later carrying a pile of rubber-impregnated yellow canvas.

"Grab a couple of fire extinguishers off the bulkheads," Hubbard ordered Laura.

By the time she had gotten the first fire extinguisher from its mount, the pile of yellow canvas was assuming the outlines of a rubber boat. By the time she returned with a second extinguisher, Pombal had it in the water, and Hubbard was handing him a small outboard motor. She looked over at the work boat.

The stream of black smoke that had been streaming up from the deck seemed to have been cut off. She saw Chet Crawford directing the stream of the large fire extinguisher onto the deck.

"The fire's out," Laura said just as Pombal bolted the outboard engine into place. He couldn't hear her because of the motor, but he followed her gestures. Then he killed the engine.

"The fire's out," Laura repeated unnecessarily.

Another voice, Chet Crawford's, was heard faintly across the expanse of water: "Get your fat ass over here, you goddamned Portugee son of a bitch!"

Hubbard and Pombal looked at each other.

"I think," Hubbard said solemnly, "that the chief would have a word with you, Seaman Pombal."

They laughed together softly, grinning from ear to ear. Then Pombal bent over and jerked the starter rope of the outboard again and then, kneeling in the stern, with the bow out of the water, crossed to the work boat.

"What happened?" Laura asked, confused.

"What I think happened," Hubbard said, his hand dropping to cup her shoulder, "is that we had a simple, ordinary, accidental fire. Which Crawford is going to try to blame on Pombal."

Laura was relieved to hear that explanation, and she was pleased with Hubbard's affectionate holding of her shoulder. She put her hand up to rest it on his and simultaneously moved against him. He instantly took his hand from her shoulder and walked into the cabin.

She stood there a moment, feeling rejected and furious, and then she walked to the cabin door.

"What are you afraid of?" she demanded angrily. "That you don't dare trust your instincts?"

She thought she was going to get a reply, but when he finally spoke, all he said was, "I'm going on deck. You want to bring me a cup of coffee?" Then he picked up the binoculars from the table and went up the ladder.

Fifteen minutes later, the rubber boat came back across the water to the *Barbara-Ann*. This time it carried Chet Crawford.

"Why did you try to burn up the Portugee's boat, Chester? He likes you," Hubbard teased. He handed Crawford a bottle of beer.

Crawford took a long pull at it.

"What they got, Skipper, is a silenced .22," Crawford said. "And a diver who knows what he's doing."

"What the hell are you talking about?" Hubbard asked.

"Well, they're still trying to scare us off," Crawford said. "He could have put holes in me instead of in that fuel tank just as easy."

"Start at the beginning," Hubbard said.

"Well, I *heard* it," Crawford said. "I didn't know what it was. Pong, pong, pong. Maybe four pongs. What he was doing was shooting holes in the tank. Son of a bitch was probably one arm up on the boat. I went and looked, but I thought that it was Pombal's boat creaking of old age. I couldn't see anything. So what he did was swim maybe fifty yards off and wait until there was maybe five gallons of diesel fuel slopping around on the deck, and then he shot a distress flare at it. I heard that. Bang. Then a big pong as the flare hit the tank, and I went out, and there the son of a bitch was, setting the goddamn diesel fuel on fire."

"You didn't see him?"

"What I was doing, Skipper, was trying to put the fucking fire out before it set off the fuel in the tank," Crawford said. "If that had got started, I never would have got the son of a bitch out."

"How did you seal the holes in the tank?" Hubbard asked.

"I didn't seal them," Crawford said. "I stuck rags in them. There's no way they can be sealed without draining the tank, and I'll be damned if I was going to pump the son of a bitch dry."

He gestured toward the work boat. Laura saw Tony Pombal steadily working some kind of pump. Then she saw something else.

"Jack!" she said, and pointed in the direction of the *Non-Deductible*. Dexter Corten was again standing at the control console of the *Shamrock*, steering it toward the *Barbara-Ann*.

In three minutes, it was off the *Barbara-Ann*'s stern, its engine idling.

"I'd like to come aboard and talk with you, Captain Hubbard," Corten called.

"Is that the son of a bitch responsible for the fire?" Chet Crawford asked loudly enough for Dexter Corten to hear.

"I saw the fire," Corten replied. "I'm glad you were able to handle the incident. Fires like that can quickly get out of hand."

"Chet," Hubbard said. "Throw Mr. Corten a line. Let's hear what he has to say."

When Corten came aboard, he put out his hand to Crawford, who, surprised, took it.

"You must be Mr. Crawford," Corten said. "Or should I say Chief Crawford? Captain Hubbard's business associate."

"OK," Hubbard said. "So you've been asking questions. I'm suitably impressed."

"So am I, Captain Hubbard," Corten began.

"You can knock off that captain business, too," Hubbard said. "If I wanted to call myself captain, I'd buy a head boat and get one those caps with the little anchors."

Corten nodded and smiled.

"What I was about to say, Mr. Hubbard, was that I was impressed when I had a few questions about you answered. Another proof that you should not rely on first impressions. If you ask the right people, you learn as I did that you have a very impressive reputation in salvage circles. As does Mr. Pombal, and as does Chief Crawford. I really didn't realize who I was dealing with the first time I spoke with you."

"Anybody who's willing to try that much flattery on me deserves a drink," Hubbard said. "What will you have, Mr. Corten?" He gestured for Corten to go into the cabin.

"I'm a bourbon drinker, Mr. Hubbard," Corten said. "Thank you."

Hubbard seated Corten at one end of the couch and himself at the other.

Laura started to sit between them, but a look in Hubbard's eyes dissuaded her.

"What we really have here," Corten said, and then interrupted himself. "I presume you've played a hand or two of stud poker, Mr. Hubbard?"

"Once or twice," Hubbard replied.

"What we had the first time we met," Corten said, "was one card down and one showing. We both had aces as hole cards. You had a deuce showing, and I had a king. So I tried to buy the pot cheap."

"And what do we have now? Did you draw another ace?" Hubbard said.

"Let's say you've got a pair of deuces showing," Corten said. "Which would take me."

"You're impressed with my reputation, you mean? That's where I got the second deuce?" Hubbard replied.

"What is this bullshit?" Chet Crawford demanded suddenly. "Are we playing some kind of fucking game?"

"Watch your goddamn foul mouth, Chet," Hubbard said angrily, and then, to Corten: "He's got a point. Why don't we get to yours?"

"Indulge me," Corten said. "Just a little longer."

"Bullshit," Chet Crawford said.

"The third cards were just dealt," Corten went on. "You got another ace in the person of Mr. Crawford and Mr. Pombal and the marking balloon. I don't know what that marking balloon really means, whether you found the plane or whether you simply want me to think you found it."

"And what did you draw?" Hubbard asked.

"I received word that Key West Salvors, equipped with a salvage license and the chart the Coast Guard made when they came to the crash site, is finally en route here," Corten said.

"And what is that, another ace for you?"

"More like a wild card," Corten said. "It depends on how I decide to play it."

"How are you going to play it?"

"I know how I'd like to play it," Corten said. "I always like to take as few chances as I have to. I'd like to buy this pot."

"OK," Hubbard said. "Now I'm getting like Chet Crawford. I've had enough of this poker bullshit, too. The pot is the attaché case. The question is, How much is that attaché case worth?"

"There are several pots, really," Corten said. "There's a quarter of a million dollar pot: Mr. Wood's insurance."

"Unless, as has been suggested to me, Mr. Wood was doing something illegal, in which case there would be no insurance," Hubbard replied.

"Let me pose a hypothetical situation to you," Corten said. "Just for the sake of argument, let's say that there is property of mine on that airplane, valuable property, property that is of far greater value to me than it would be to anyone else. Now, Key West Salvors are people of good reputation, and they know me as a reputable businessman. Now suppose that I had gone to Key West Salvors and told them that all I really want out of that airplane is, say, an attaché case but that I am prepared, because I can deduct it as a business expense, to pay them to bring up Art Wood's body, too. A gesture of practical sympathy toward the widow of a man who died in my employ.

"Hypothetically, let us assume they find the plane and the case and the body. They give me the case because it's got my initials on it, and they don't look in it because what's in it is none of their business. And they produce the body, and because they don't want to get involved in anything that's none of their business, that's the end of it. Mrs. Wood gets her insurance payment, I get my attaché case, and you get twenty-five thousand dollars."

"Why would you want to pay me that much?"

"Because I would much rather have it known that

Key West Salvors found my property and Arthur Wood's body than you. No one is going to question their integrity. On the other hand, if it became public knowledge that someone like me had hired someone like you, I'm very afraid that eyebrows would be raised and questions posed."

"OK," Hubbard said, surprising everybody. "You've got a deal."

"How do we know he'll bring Art's body up?" Laura protested.

"Because there's no way they can get the attaché case without seeing Art's body," Hubbard said. "And Key West is as straight as an arrow. If they see the body, they'll recover it."

"And what," Laura asked, somewhat desperately, "if Art was doing something he shouldn't have been doing? And I lose out on the insurance?"

"Mrs. Wood," Dexter Corten said, "you have my word that Art was doing nothing illegal by coming out to the *Non-Deductible*. There is nothing on that plane that could be even wildly construed as illegal."

"You have a deal," Hubbard said. "Cash in advance, of course. We'll leave first thing in the morning."

"I don't have twenty-five thousand dollars in cash," Corten said. "Nobody has that much money."

"Then you can give me a check. And when the check clears the bank in Fort Meyers, I'll get on the radio and tell Key West Salvors where they can find the plane."

"You really did find it?" Corten said, taking a checkbook from his pocket.

"I really found it," Hubbard said. "I drew two aces to my hole ace."

"Jesus," Chet Crawford said in disgust. "We're back to the poker bullshit."

"Well," Dexter Corten said, "there doesn't seem to be anything else to say, does there?"

"I can't think of anything," Hubbard said.

"Then I might as well get back to the *Non-Deductible*," Corten announced. "Would you like to come for dinner?"

"I think I'd better stay aboard," Hubbard said. "Thank you just the same."

Corten stepped over the rail and started down the ladder to the swim platform.

"I hope you had the battery charged," Hubbard said.

"I replaced the battery," Corten said. "I don't like to take chances." He got into the *Shamrock* and started the engine. He stood at the console for a moment with his hand on the transmission control, obviously deep in thought, and then he pushed the transmission control forward. Water boiled up behind the *Shamrock*, and then the boat moved quickly away from the *Barbara-Ann*.

Hubbard went up the ladder to the upper deck, opened a chest, and took out two small pennants. He ran them up the *Barbara-Ann*'s mast. On one pennant was a representation of a hot dog impaled on a stick; on the other was a martini glass.

"Jesus!" Crawford said disgustedly. But the pennants served their intended purpose. A moment later, Laura saw Tony Pombal shove the flat-bottomed dinghy into the water and climb into it. He started the engine, and the dinghy started across the water to the *Barbara-Ann*.

"So what's going on?" Tony Pombal asked over his shoulder as he headed for the half-gallon bottle of bourbon on the table.

"That's what I'd like to know," Laura said just loudly enough for Hubbard to hear.

"The man had a very convincing story," Hubbard said. "He says that his attaché case is in the airplane. I saw an attaché case in the airplane. He is worried that the contents of the attaché case may embarrass him. Which is different, I think, than seeing him go to jail.

So what I think is that there is money in the attaché case, not cocaine. If it came out, if the IRS heard, or the Bureau of Narcotics and Dangerous Drugs, or for that matter the Fort Myers newspaper heard that Dexter Corten had a whole lot of money in an attaché case, questions would be asked. If I was trying to hide a million dollars from the IRS, I would pay to keep it hidden. Twenty-five thousand to us plus whatever Key West Salvors charge him, say, another twenty-five, is only five percent of a million dollars.''

"So you trust him?"

"Not at all," Hubbard said. "But I don't think he knows the plane was blown up. He wouldn't be so anxious to have Key West Salvors find it if he did."

"What's going to happen when they find out it was blown up?" Laura asked.

"An investigation, of course," Hubbard said. "And publicity. Which works to Laura's advantage, not against it. Maybe Corten can get his attaché case back, and maybe he can't. But we're out of it with twenty-five thousand dollars for our trouble. And unless Fallon can prove that Art Wood blew himself up, they're going to have to pay off."

"The Coast Guard's going to ask you questions," Pombal said. "What are you going to tell them?"

"The truth," Hubbard said. "That after I found the plane, Corten came to me and offered me twenty-five thousand dollars to go home."

"Why would he want to do that?" Pombal asked.

"You'll have to ask him that," Hubbard said.

"And why did you take it?" Pombal asked. Laura suddenly understood what was going on. Tony Pombal was playing devil's advocate, trying to find flaws in Hubbard's reasoning.

"Because it seemed the smart thing to do," Hubbard said. "Key West Salvors are a reputable, well-equipped salvage firm, much better equipped to raise an airplane than you are with the rusty little boat of yours. And twenty-five thousand dollars is found money for a bunch of guys who came here out of the goodness of their hearts to help the widow of a guy who had saved their lives in Nam.''

"You're a devious bastard, Skipper," Pombal said after thinking it over.

"Ain't I?" Hubbard said, smiling, pleased with himself.

"I got one," Crawford said. " 'Hubbard, are you telling me you didn't see that plane had been in an explosion?' "

"Sure," Hubbard said, quoting himself. "I guess it blew up when it crashed."

" 'And what, if anything, did you see in the cockpit?' "

"I didn't take a good look," Hubbard said. "The crabs were working on the body."

"Oh, my God," Laura said.

"Sorry," Hubbard said.

"Jesus, Jack," Pombal grunted in disapproval.

"Any more questions?" Hubbard asked.

"No," Pombal said. "That's more than enough. Let's eat."

Laura, white-faced, ran into the master's cabin.

CHAPTER
16

It was dark when Laura Wood opened the door to the cabin. She was wearing the terrycloth blouse and slacks and had her arms crossed across her chest, under her breasts, as if she were chilled. When Hubbard looked across the cabin at her, he could see her breasts, nipples erect, in his mind's eye.

Hubbard was sitting at the table. Under the light of a high-intensity lamp, he was in the process of reassembling a very large fishing reel. There was the smell of a miracle lubricant in the air. Beside the frame of the fishing reel was the snubnose Smith & Wesson.

"I thought maybe you'd get hungry," Hubbard said. "But I didn't want to wake you up."

"I only heard one outboard," she said. "Is somebody still here?"

"They both went back in the dinghy," he said. He gestured toward the cockpit. The inflatable boat had been brought aboard.

"Oh."

"Listen," he said. "I'm really sorry about what I said before, about the crabs down there in the airplane. It just slipped out."

She nodded. "It's OK, Jack."

"We made you a steak," he said. "It's cold, but . . ."

"Come to bed, Jack," Laura said. She turned and went back in the master's cabin. There was enough light from the cabin for him to see her slip out of the slacks and then pull the terrycloth blouse over her head. Then she turned around so that she was facing him.

He stood up and picked up the revolver and went to her.

Laura woke when she sensed Hubbard moving away from her. They had been sleeping entwined, on their left sides, Hubbard's arm around her, his fingers brushing her breast.

He moves like a snake, she thought, or like an Indian in the forest. There was only the faintest movement of the mattress as he left the bed, and not a sound. She listened intently for the sound of his movement in the cabin and heard nothing. Then she waited for the sound of him in the head, where he had probably gone to empty his bladder. She heard nothing but a creaking that could have been anything. When she heard no sound from the head, she decided that he had gone out into the cabin, possibly up to the upper deck to have a look around. He would be back, she told herself. He would get back in the bed as stealthily as he had left it, and his arm would gently go around hers again, and he would ever so gently again cup her breast and go back to sleep again, snuggled up close and warm next to her.

She heard the cabin door squeak just barely audibly. He was coming back. She wondered why she hadn't heard the door squeak as he went out.

The light in the cabin suddenly came on, hurting her eyes. There was a man standing just inside the door, covered except for his face and hands in a black rubber wet suit. She sat up in terror, oblivious to her nakedness, and sucked in her breath audibly. When he pushed the breathing apparatus out of the way so that she could see his face and his smile, she put her balled fists before her mouth and whimpered.

"For Christ's sake, Laura," the man said, "don't scream. You'll wake the neighbors. Where's your boy friend?"

"Right here, Wood," Hubbard's voice came from the closet. "Move an eyebrow and I'll blow your fucking head off!"

Laura snapped her head behind her to look at the closet. The folding doors were cracked open just wide enough for Hubbard to get both his hands through. All she could see at first was his hands and the .38 pistol they held. Then the right door slid open farther, and Hubbard stepped out. His nakedness reminded Laura of her own, and she reached down and pulled the sheet up over her breasts.

Art Wood raised his hands above his head.

"No gun," he said, smiling. "No knife, nothing."

"Stand there," Hubbard ordered. He crossed the room quickly to him, spun him around, and put the barrel of the gun against his face. The muzzle pressed into black rubber over the soft flesh where the jaw meets the throat. He twisted Wood's arm behind him and raised his voice. "Wood gets blown away if anybody so much as twitches."

Then he pushed Wood through the door into the cabin. No more than a minute later, he pushed him roughly back into the cabin.

"There's nobody else," Hubbard said to Laura. He let Wood's arm go. Wood looked at Laura.

"What happened to your titty, honey?" Arthur Wood asked, indicating the bandage on his wife's breast. "Old Jack get carried away?"

Hubbard, furious, spun Wood around and raised his hand.

"Jack," Laura heard herself say, "don't!"

Hubbard grabbed the harness of Wood's breathing apparatus and pulled Wood's face close to his.

"What the hell is going on, you son of a bitch?" Hubbard demanded. Then he pushed Wood violently backward so that he fell into the upholstered chair.

"That's my line, Jack," Art Wood said. "What you're supposed to say is, 'There's an explanation for this' or something like that."

"Well," Hubbard said, "I'll say this for you, for somebody with his balls in a crack, you're pretty goddamn nonchalant."

"You're the one whose balls are in a crack," Wood said. "I'm here to save your ass. Again."

"Shit," Hubbard said.

"It's God's truth, Jack," Wood told him. "You're going to have to hear me out."

Hubbard looked at Laura, and she was so frightened at the look in his eyes that it was a moment before she understood what he was thinking.

"Jack, I didn't know . . ."

"She didn't know, Jack," Arthur Wood said. "How the hell could I trust her?" he added reasonably.

"Put your clothes on," Hubbard said to Laura. She tugged the sheet loose from the foot of the bed.

"Don't mind me," Wood said. "I've seen it all before."

Laura wrapped the sheet around her and then moved with her back to the cabin wall to the head, squatting quickly en route to pick up the blouse and slacks where she had dropped them.

When she came back in the cabin, Hubbard had put on his shirt and was holding the revolver in his armpit as he zipped his trousers. When she looked at her husband, she saw that the top of the lower portion of the wet suit had been pulled down below his knees. He would not, she understood, be able to walk, much less rush across the cabin hobbled that way.

When Laura looked at Hubbard, she found his eyes already on hers.

"I don't know whether to tell you to stay away from him so he can't grab you or tell you to go sit on his lap where I can keep my eye on both of you at once," Hubbard said.

Laura bit her lip. She moaned. She said Hubbard's name and began to cry.

"That won't do it," Arthur Wood said. "I don't think tears will work on Jack."

"Shut your goddamn mouth," Hubbard said, and then, gently, to Laura: "I'm sorry I said that."

"It's all right," Laura said.

She looked at him, and he made a small gesture with his hand, enough for her to interpret it as in invitation to come to him. When she got close, he held his arm higher, and she put her arms around him and put her face against his chest for a moment. Then she turned around and faced her husband.

"Very touching," Arthur Wood said sarcastically. "Apparently this was bigger than both of you."

"You bastard," Laura said bitterly. "How could you do this to Little Art?"

"My intention was to leave Little Art's mother with a quarter of a million dollars," Arthur Wood said. "Which is a lot more than most men do when they check out."

"Why?" Laura demanded.

Arthur Wood shrugged his shoulders.

"Who's in the plane?" Hubbard asked.

"Nobody anybody's going to miss, much less look for," Wood said. "An ungrateful, spiteful little bitch."

"Interesting choice of words," Hubbard said. "A very dear friend of yours, no doubt?"

The confirmation came a moment after Laura had the first incredible suspicion? "Don't knock it till you try it," Wood said.

"OK," Hubbard said. "What do you want here?"

"By the time Key West Salvors get here in the morning," Arthur Wood said, "I want Mr. Dexter Corten gone. I want you to terminate him by extreme means."

Hubbard just looked at him.

"That's the phrase, isn't it, that all your swashbucklers used, 'terminate by extreme means'?" Wood asked.

"You're out of your mind, Art," Hubbard said matter-of-factly.

"No," Wood replied. "I'm not. Not at all. I'm thinking very clearly. More clearly than I think I ever have before."

"I'm not going to terminate anybody for you," Hubbard said.

"Kill or be killed, Jack," Arthur Wood said. "You, Pombal, Crawford, and, of course, my wife. It's going to have to be either him or you, all of you."

"Why would Dexter Corten want to kill us?"

"Because he will think that you have his million two hundred and thirty thousand dollars," Art Wood said. "And for that kind of money, he'll kill. Take my word for it."

"I don't have his money," Hubbard said. "If you're talking about the attaché case in the airplane, he'll have that back just as soon as they bring the airplane up. Dexter Corten has no quarrel with us. With you maybe, but not with us."

"The attaché case is there?" Wood asked. "In one piece?"

"Yes. It's on the floor of the plane. The plane is on its back."

"I was sort of hoping that explosion would get the attaché case," Wood said. "Sort of scatter the contents."

"You should have used more dynamite," Hubbard said.

"I was sort of hoping that it would look like a natural explosion."

"You shouldn't get into things where you don't know what you're doing," Hubbard told him.

"Neither should you, Jack," Wood said. "The mess you're in is your own fault."

"I still don't understand what mess you're talking about," Hubbard said.

"I told you," Wood said. "When they bring the attaché case up and find that there's no money in it, Corten is going to draw the obvious conclusion that you have it. You found the plane. You're the only one who's had the opportunity."

"Well, let me lay it out for you, Art," Hubbard said. "For one thing, I don't have any explosives, so I couldn't blow up his boat. And I couldn't just go over there and blow him away, because he's not alone, and I couldn't get within fifty feet of him carrying a weapon. And finally, I don't take out people just because they might get mad at me for something I didn't do. What you have to worry about is me getting on the radio and telling Dexter Corten who's sitting in my cabin."

That apparently was a possibility that Arthur Wood had not thought of. He felt a moment's contempt for Wood. But then he remembered the attempt to take the *Barbara-Ann* off Panama City and the men who had tried to kill him on the wharf in Fort Myers, and the contempt gave way to a cold anger.

"Be reasonable, Jack," Wood said, having thought of a new tack. "We can all come out of this with what we want. Safely. Everybody home free."

"You get all the money, right, and I get her?" Hubbard said, nodding at Laura. "Is that what you're seriously proposing?"

Wood forced a laugh.

"Make me a counterproposal," he said.

"I'll take the two hundred and thirty thousand you mentioned," Hubbard said.

Wood made a show of considering this.

"I'm not in this alone," he said.

"Well, then, why don't you and I just swim over and ask Mr. Fallon?" Hubbard said.

"Jack, you can't seriously—" Laura began.

"It's like they say about hookers, honey," Arthur Wood interrupted her. "Everybody does it. Some people charge more than others."

"What I want you to do," Hubbard said coldly to Laura, "is give me thirty minutes. If I'm not back in thirty minutes, you start blowing the horn. And when Pombal and Crawford get here, you tell them exactly what happened. Exactly."

She looked at him without saying anything.

"Do what I tell you, damn it," Hubbard said.

"You see, I'm not the only one who thinks women should do what they're told," Wood said.

"Don't push your luck, Wood," Hubbard said. "Let's go." He handed Laura the revolver. "You don't have to do anything but point it and pull the trigger."

"I don't want it," she said.

"Suit yourself," Hubbard said. "You'll do your kid a lot of good if you get your throat cut." He turned to Wood. "Let's go."

"Aren't you going to suit up?"

"I don't need diving gear to swim two hundred yards without being seen," Hubbard said. He walked to the cockpit, went down the ladder to the swim platform, and slipped into the water.

Laura saw that the current had turned all three boats so that the stern of the *Barbara-Ann* could not be seen from the others.

"I don't suppose you'll believe this," Arthur Wood said to her, "but I really tried not to get you involved in this."

She looked into his eyes for a moment and then looked away.

Arthur Wood put the mouthpiece of the breathing apparatus into his mouth and went down the ladder to the swim platform.

She could follow the trail of his bubbles for a moment, but then that too was gone.

Hubbard surfaced just long enough to get a breath and his bearings and then slipped silently below the surface again. He swam under the large boat and came up beside the hull. He put his hand on the splash board and listened.

"I think that's him," a voice he did not recognize said.

There was a faint splashing, and he could detect movement of the boat. Wood had reached the boat and was about to go on board. The proof came when the boat moved unmistakably.

"Well?" Fallon asked.

"He's coming here."

There was the sound of something metallic bumping the deck. That's Wood, Hubbard thought, taking off his tanks. He let go of the splash board, sank far enough beneath the surface so that he could turn over in the water, and then swam thirty feet away and surfaced. He took a noisy breath and then softly called Wood's name.

"Hello again, Mr. Hubbard," Fallon called softly.

Hubbard swam on the surface to the stern of the large boat. There was no swim platform, but a chain ladder hung from the railing. Hubbard put his hand on it. He looked up. Fallon was leaning over the stern, prepared to help him aboard.

Hubbard pulled himself up the first several steps until his feet found the submerged part of the ladder. He climbed onto the boat.

The man whose life Hubbard had spared by uncollapsing his larynx on the wharf in Fort Myers was standing on the deck with a large fire ax, in a position to swing it.

If he had wanted to kill me, he would have used that thing on me when I was coming up the ladder, whether or not I had taken Fallon's offered arm.

Arthur Wood, his tanks still strapped to his back, was lying on the deck. There was blood coming out of his nose and mouth. His eyes were open, and he was dead.

He hit him with the flat side of that ax, not with the blade or the point. I was right about that son of a bitch; he's a professional.

Fallon used the very word to him.

"You are a professional, aren't you, Mr. Hubbard?" Fallon said. "You didn't even look surprised."

"I was surprised."

"This is more in your line of expertise than mine," Fallon said. "How would you dispose of that?" He pointed to Wood's body.

"You need about four hundred pounds to weigh something like that down so it won't rise when it turns gaseous," Hubbard said. "But you could probably use half that much weight, that much anchor chain, if you had some to spare, tied to his legs with fishing line. The current here would probably carry it forty, fifty miles before it came to the surface, and by that time the sharks and the barracudas would probably have gotten most of it."

Fallon nodded. "Thank you," he said. "Let's go in the cabin. We have to talk."

"We can talk here," Hubbard said. "I can be back in the water before he can get at me with that ax."

"Tell Mr. Hubbard what I told you," Fallon said.

"I'm supposed to keep you alive so he can talk to you," the man croaked.

"Sore throat?" Hubbard asked.

"I owe you, shitface," the man croaked.

"You owe me your life," Hubbard said.

"Shit!"

"Oh, I'm sure Mr. Hubbard wouldn't say that unless he meant it," Fallon said. "The reason I suggested we go inside is so that we won't be on display."

"I'm not going to give you that much of an advantage,'' Hubbard said reasonably.

"Put the ax on the deck and give Mr. Hubbard your pistol," Fallon ordered. "Butt first, like in the cowboy movies.''

There was disbelief and a hint of mutiny in the man's eyes.

"Mr. Hubbard," Fallon said reasonably, "doesn't kill people unless he has a good reason. You should know that. And I don't intend to give any reason at all.'' Then his voice changed. "Give him the goddamn gun," he said coldly.

The man, with great reluctance, took a stainless-steel pistol from the small of his back and handed it butt first to Hubbard. Hubbard quickly worked the action. The gun was already loaded, and a cartridge flew through the air and landed on the deck.

Hubbard raised the pistol and, steadying his right elbow with his left hand, aimed it at the bridge of the nose of the man who had just given it to him.

"On your knees, asshole," he said.

The man nervously licked his lips and looked at Fallon for help.

"He can't help you," Hubbard said reasonably. He started to count. By the time he got to two, the man was on his knees.

CHAPTER
17

"Put your hands behind your head," Hubbard ordered. The man looked at Fallon again but then put out his hands behind his head.

"Stick out your tongue," Hubbard ordered.

The man looked at him in disbelief.

"Stick out your tongue," Hubbard ordered brutally.

The man stuck out his tongue.

Hubbard lowered the pistol so that it hung at his side. Then he laughed.

Fallon joined in. "You had nothing to worry about," he said to the man on his knees. "Mr. Hubbard is a reasonable man."

"You go in the cabin first," Hubbard said to the man on his knees. "And then you, Fallon, and I'll just stay close to the door."

In the cabin, Hubbard ordered the man who had held the ax to lie on his stomach on the deck with his hands in his hip pockets.

"You're very careful," Fallon said. "It's unnecessary."

"It's always necessary," Hubbard said.

Fallon nodded agreement. "What did Wood tell you?" he asked.

"What was he supposed to tell me?"

"He was supposed to kill you," Fallon said.

"You should have known that men like Wood can't kill."

"If he had, he would be alive and you would be dead," Fallon told him.

"Why did you kill him now?" Hubbard asked.

"Because he couldn't be trusted."

"Why didn't you try to kill me?"

"Because, under proper circumstances, you can be."

"There is no honor among thieves, Fallon. You were a cop; you should know that better than anybody."

"How about enlightened self-interest?" Fallon replied.

"I want to know what's going on around here," Hubbard said. "And I don't want any bullshit."

"I really hadn't intended to hand you any," Fallon said.

"What about the bullshit you tried to hand me on the boat in Fort Myers?"

"That was no bullshit," Fallon said. "If you had accepted that offer and brought up the body and proof that Art Wood was doing something illegal, my company would have happily paid you the thirty thousand I offered."

"And the presence of the cops would have scared Dexter Corten off?"

"Mr. Corten would have come to the conclusion that you had helped yourself to his money. Since Art was dead, there was no way he could have come up with any connection to me."

"But Art wasn't dead. And who's in the plane?"

"Let me start at the beginning," Fallon said. "Arthur Wood first came to my attention when he arranged for his car to be stolen. He is not a very clever thief, but you don't have to be to pull that off, once. He attracted my curiosity because he was a pilot, and when pilots in lower Florida get desperate for money, they generally make a trip or two to Colombia. A fraudulent insurance claim for a stolen car is grand larceny and will get you three to five. A trip to Colombia is a much safer way to break the law and pays a hell of a lot more.

"So I wonder about this guy. When you're a cop as long as I was, you get a feeling about people. So I checked him out. And the reason he doesn't make trips to Colombia is because he's working for Corten, and Corten doesn't want him to do that. So why, if he's working for Corten, does he need money?"

"The boyfriend?" Hubbard asked levelly.

"Right. He's maintaining two households, and the boyfriend has expensive tastes."

"So why doesn't he move out on his wife? That wouldn't be the first time."

"Because if he did, that would be the end of him with Corten. Corten is Mr. Respectable. He doesn't want people saying that the guy who flies him around is the faggot who left his wife and little boy for a boy."

"What does Corten do?" Hubbard asked.

"I don't really know," Fallon admitted.

"Come on," Hubbard said disbelievingly.

"I really don't," Fallon said. "All I know for sure is that he takes money out of the country. Now whether this money is used to pay for drugs in Colombia or whether it's the profits that he's got some way of sanitizing, I don't know. And I didn't really want to ask too many questions."

"Tell me something, Fallon," Hubbard said. "What do you know about the guys who tried to take my boat?"

"I guess I should have told them who you were," Fallon said matter-of-factly. "Then they would have done a better job."

"If I had turned up missing, with Mrs. Wood," Hubbard said, "Corten would have spent a lot of time looking for me and his money, right?"

"That's right," Fallon admitted.

"The guys who tried to take my boat in on this scam?" Hubbard asked.

Fallon shook his head. "Sometimes," he said, "what the company will pay to get an insured yacht back is more than the bad guys can get for it. You meet interesting people in my line of work."

"What I'd really like to know is how the hell I got involved," Hubbard asked.

"You weren't supposed to be," Fallon said. "The way it was supposed to go down was simplicity itself. Wood picks up the money. Wood lands, and we take the money out of the briefcase, and the boyfriend gets in."

"Tell me about that?"

"The boyfriend is not faithful. I have pictures. Hell hath no fury like a cuckolded faggot."

"And you've got the dynamite rigged to the low-altitude warning system?"

"Something like that."

"Two-level detonation. Low-altitude circuit triggers trembler switch?"

"You're good," Fallon said appreciatively. "You would have made a good cop."

"The plane blows and sinks, the boyfriend gets buried as Art Wood, and if Corten doesn't swallow the story that his money went down with the fishes, he doesn't know where to look anyway, right?"

"Right."

"Flying money out to a boat may be unusual, but it's not illegal," Hubbard said.

"There was supposed to be a hundred grand worth of cocaine on the plane," Fallon said.

"You're good," Hubbard said. "Let Corten explain that to the cops. But you said was."

"Art Wood was a greedy shit. He figured a hundred grand was a hundred grand."

"You found it?"

"When he was over trying to kill you," Fallon said. "He didn't have a chance to get rid of it. He's been on the boat ever since his boy friend swapped places with him."

"And I sort of screwed up your plans when Mrs. Wood came to me?"

"You could have been useful," Fallon said. "If those boat guys had gotten you, that would have led Corten on a wild chase. And if you had taken my offer, that would have been useful. And if they had managed to do what I sent them to do on the wharf, that would have been useful. And if Wood had killed you tonight, that would have been useful."

"And now I'm going to cost you money."

"There's no free lunch, Hubbard. You know that."

"If I blow up Corten's boat, I'm going to be suspected of it."

"No. Think it through. You're the good guy, coming to the rescue of the poor widow. They can't tie you to Corten because you never heard the name until Mrs. Wood came to you. Why should you blow him up? The same people who blew up the airplane, drug people, blew up the yacht. Happens all the time."

Hubbard looked at him but said nothing.

"How would you go about blowing up a boat like that?" Fallon said. "Specifically, I mean?"

"It's not easy without the proper equipment," Hubbard said.

"What I've got is nineteen sticks of dynamite," Fallon said, "and a box of detonators, I don't know how many. If there was a dozen in it, we used two."

"We're getting ahead of ourselves," Hubbard said. "We get to the question of what's in it for me."

"You don't have Corten looking for his money, which he'll think you have if he's around when they bring up that airplane tomorrow and it's not there."

"I'm going to have some of his money," Hubbard said.

"Is that so?"

"That's so."

"I'm a reasonable man," Fallon said. "How much?"

"I've had a bad run at the track lately," Hubbard said. "I could come up with a hundred and twenty-five thousand without making the IRS suspicious of where I got it."

"You're a horse player?" Fallon asked. "You don't seem the type."

"Sometimes you can't tell about people," Hubbard said. "Can you?"

"Call it a hundred thousand even," Fallon said.

"Call it a hundred and twenty-five thousand," Hubbard said.

"You've got a deal."

"I want the money," Hubbard said. "In God I trust. All others pay cash."

"You don't think I have it here, do you?"

"Yes, as a matter of fact, I do," Hubbard said.

"The Coast Guard's going to be here," Fallon said. "What if they search your boat?"

"The Coast Guard has searched my boat before," Hubbard said, and closed the subject by saying, "I hope you've got some plastic garbage bags."

"Yeah, there's some. I saw some."

"This is gasoline, isn't it?" Hubbard asked. "Gasoline works a lot better than diesel fuel. And I'll need that CB radio and the battery from that lantern and some line."

"You're going to do this alone?" Fallon asked.

"If I asked my friends to help me," Hubbard said. "There would be two more people with information and two people who'd want some of the money."

Fallon looked at him and smiled.

"You're really something, Hubbard," he said. "Really something."

Hubbard swam on the surface for fifty yards, very slowly and quietly towing the plastic bags behind him.

When he was as far away from the boat as he thought he could safely go underwater, he sank beneath the surface and swam to it.

He was almost out of breath when his hand touched the hull, and it took all his willpower not to exhale noisily when he broke the surface but instead to exhale and inhale silently and painfully. His temples throbbed with the manifestations of oxygen starvation, but it passed.

He went under the boat, found the propeller shaft, and quickly tied everything in place. Then he went back to the surface carefully so that there would be no splashing when he came up.

This was the hardest part, the silent swimming, the coming up silently, the controlling of his breathing.

The rest of it he had done before, and now he did it with practiced ease in six dives. He lashed the twisted, closed necks of the plastic garbage bags, three of them, each holding about two gallons of gasoline, to the propeller shaft. They were buoyant, for gas is lighter than water, and once their necks had been lashed to the propeller shaft, buoyancy raised them against the hull and molded them to the curved hull.

The dynamite in its plastic bag with the battery and the detonators was not buoyant. He lashed it to the propeller shaft below where the plastic gasoline bags were tied.

The last step was uncoiling the wire he had rigged between the detonators and the CB radio as he carefully rose for the last time to the surface. He had rigged the signal strength meter so that instead of moving the needle on the face of the instrument, the electrical impulse would trigger the detonators.

As soon as he turned the CB radio on, the dynamite would be detonated whenever a signal was received on channel 25. Any signal on channel 25 would set it off. His only safety factor was a length of copper wire he had rigged as an antenna. It was not, he hoped, going to prove to be a very good antenna. All it had to do was pick up the keying of the mike on the CB in the boat. If it picked up the signal of some fisherman talking to his buddy or a skip signal bounced off the ionosphere, it would set off the dynamite, and that would be the end of him.

He had spent five minutes in the water, with Fallon watching him as if he didn't believe what he was seeing, achieving negative buoyancy between the weight of the CB radio and the amount of air in the two plastic garbage bags that protected it from the sea water. He'd succeeded, but that had been before he'd swum fifty yards on the surface and then another fifty under the water, and air could have escaped, or the bags could have been torn.

But when he let the CB radio loose, it moved sluggishly to the surface and stayed there. The antenna bag floated loosely and evenly on the surface. He pulled the CB bag to him, turned the radio on, and let it go again.

Then he took as deep a breath as he could manage, slipped under the water, and started swimming.

The black object sailed over the railing and landed at the feet of the lookout Dexter Corten had stationed in the cockpit of the *Non-Deductible*.

The lookout had been leaning on the rail, taking yet another look at the *Barbara-Ann* and the *Shamrock* and the battered work boat.

He spun around with a pistol in his hand. "What the fuck?" he said.

For a moment, he thought that it was a flying fish, but then he saw that it was a plastic garbage bag. In his nervousness, he had aimed his pistol at it.

"Shit," he said, and walked to it and kicked at it tentatively.

"Mr. Corten," he called. In a moment, Dexter Corten appeared, followed by Frazier. "I don't know what the hell this is," the lookout said. "It came over the side."

"Jesus Christ, a bomb," Frazier said.

"Don't be absurd," Dexter Corten said. He took a boat hook from a rack and pushed on the bag and then picked it up.

"There's something inside," he said. He got on his knees and ripped the bag open.

"I'll be damned," he said. "There's money in here."

He picked up a lantern, walked to the railing, and shined it on the surface of the water.

"It's Hubbard," Hubbard called. "Put that damned lamp out."

The light went out, and Hubbard swam to the *Non-Deductible*'s stern and climbed up onto the swim platform.

"If there's a light up there," he said, "turn it out. I don't want Fallon to see me."

In a moment, the light went off. Hubbard climbed the ladder and went into the *Non-Deductible*'s cockpit. The lookout, waiting for him, knocked his feet out from under him and sent him sprawling.

"Call your goon off me, Corten," Hubbard shouted.

"Let him get up," Corten ordered after a moment.

"Up, hell, I'm going to crawl across the deck into the cabin," Hubbard said. He did so.

When he was inside the cabin, Corten closed the door, and Hubbard got to his feet.

Another man, the fourth man he had seen through his binoculars, had been asleep on a couch. He sat up and shook his head and looked curiously at Hubbard.

"What the hell is all this about?" Corten asked.

"If I had meant you any harm, I wouldn't have called out to you," Hubbard said. "Tell your goon to put that gun down."

Corten gestured to the lookout.

"Did you find the money?" Hubbard asked.

"Yes," Corten said.

"I don't want any part of your feud with Fallon," Hubbard said.

"I don't even know the man," Corten said.

"Well, he's got your money," Hubbard said. "And he just gave me one hundred twenty-five thousand dollars to blow up your boat."

"What kind of a story is that?"

"Count the goddamn money," Hubbard said. "Where would I get that kind of money?"

"There's that much in here, Dexter," Frazier said. "I didn't count it exactly, but there's a hundred thousand or so in here."

"What the hell is going on?" Corten asked rhetorically.

"I don't know, but I don't want any part of it," Hubbard said.

"What exactly did this man say to you?" Corten asked.

"He told me that when they bring the airplane up, they're not going to find an attaché case on it, and when that happens, you're going to think I've got it, and unless I blew up your boat, I stood a very good chance of getting myself killed by you."

"And you believed this story?"

"When I saw the attaché case full of money, I damned well did," Hubbard said.

"You saw the money?" Corten asked.

"There's part of it," Hubbard said. "Jesus, what kind of proof do you need?"

"How the hell did he get it?" Corten asked, and then answered his own question. "Unless it was never on the goddamn airplane."

"How come you have this?" Frazier asked Hubbard, gesturing to the money.

"That's what he paid me to blow you up," Hubbard said.

"Are there divers on that boat?" Frazier asked.

"I don't know," Hubbard said. "If there were, he

would have had them blow you up, probably.''

"What's your angle in this?"

"I've got your check," Hubbard said. "And I want to stay alive."

"You want to stay alive?" Corten asked.

"I want to go back to my boat," Hubbard said. "And get the hell out of here, but I can't do that unless you do something about Fallon."

Corten looked thoughtful a moment.

"You're not going anywhere," he said. "You're going to stay right here. We're going to have a talk with Fallon."

"Hey, I did right by you," Hubbard said.

"My impulse right now is to break your arms and legs and throw you over the side," Corten said. "So don't open your mouth one more time."

"I think he has to go," Frazier said.

"Not right now," Corten said. "First we go talk to Fallon."

"He already knows too much," Frazier said.

"He doesn't know anything that can hurt us," Corten said. "And there's a million dollars involved. Whatever we do to him can wait thirty minutes."

Corten went to a drawer in a cabinet and took out a revolver. He put it into his pocket and went out into the cockpit.

"Let's go," he said to Frazier. He turned to the others. "You two watch this guy like a hawk."

He went down the ladder and got into the *Shamrock*. Frazier followed him. Corten started the *Shamrock*'s engine. Hubbard walked to the cabin door.

"Back in there, you," the lookout snapped at Hubbard.

"You've got the guns," Hubbard said, stopping and putting his hands up.

There was the sudden report of a pistol being fired.

"What the fuck?" the lookout said. The *Shamrock* swerved violently and then straightened.

"What that was," Hubbard said, "was Frazier shooting Corten."

"Bullshit," the lookout said.

"You've got a light," Hubbard said. "Use it."

The other man grabbed a storage battery-powered flashlight and turned it on. The beam cut through the darkness and stopped on the *Shamrock*. Hubbard looked over his shoulder at the light. Dexter Corten was nowhere in sight.

"Jesus Christ," the lookout said.

"Maybe that insurance guy shot him," the other one said.

"Then why is Frazier heading right for the boat?" Hubbard asked.

"You tell me, wise guy," the lookout said.

"Because Frazier and the insurance guy stole Corten's money," Hubbard said. "And Corten was just about to find that out."

"He's sure as hell going on the big boat," the second man said.

Hubbard went into the cabin and crossed to the interior communications panel. He turned on the CB, cranked the channel selector to 25, and pressed the microphone switch.

The stern of the big boat lifted out of the water. A moment later, six gallons of gasoline converted to vapor by seven sticks of dynamite detonated. There was a ball of orange fire thirty-feet across, in the light of which parts of the boat, blown fifty yards into the sky, could be seen.

A moment later, parts of the boat crashed down onto the roof of the *Non-Deductible*, and then there was the sound of water falling like rain on the cabin roof. Two of the cabin windows exploded inward, and a moment after that, there was a large splash right off the stern as something large fell out of the sky into the water.

The two men, who had been awestruck by the explosion, suddenly remembered Hubbard. Guns drawn, they came into the cabin.

"You better have some answers," the larger one said.

"I have no idea what happened," Hubbard said. "And neither do you. You don't know what happened any more than I do."

"Yeah, bullshit," the larger one said.

"While one of you divides that hundred and twenty-five thousand into three equal piles," Hubbard said, "I am going to get on the radio and call the Coast Guard and tell them there has been an explosion. Then I'm going to pick up one of those piles and put it back in the bag and swim back to my boat. And when the Coast Guard comes, I'm going to tell them I don't know what happened."

"What if we just put a couple of holes in you and feed you to the fishes?"

"Then my friends will insist that the Coast Guard search for me, and they'll find the money, and you'll have to explain where it came from and why it doesn't belong to Corten's estate. If you're lucky, the Coast Guard will find my body and charge you with murder and complicity before my friends get to you."

Hubbard could see Laura Wood standing in the cockpit of the *Barbara-Ann* as he swam up to it.

There had been the glow of flames, but at that moment it died. Hubbard stopped swimming and began to tread water as he searched for the large boat. There was nothing on the surface of the water. The boat was gone.

He didn't think the Coast Guard would search for long.

Old gasoline-powered, wooden-hulled cabin cruisers had a nasty habit of blowing up.

He resumed swimming.

Laura Wood didn't say anything when he pulled himself onto the swim platform or at first when he climbed into the cockpit. Then she said, "Are you all right?"

"Fallon's thug killed Art," Hubbard said.

"That's not what I asked, Jack," Laura said.

"They weighed his body down so that the current will

take it away," Hubbard went on. "By the time they find it, if they find it, there won't be enough left of it to tell it from the body in the airplane."

There was horror in her eyes, but she didn't say anything.

He went to her and put his hands on her arms and looked for a long moment into her eyes.

"If they bury the body in the airplane as Art," he said, "the insurance company will pay his policy. Double indemnity."

She nodded her head dully and then looked up into his eyes.

"Has your little boy ever ridden a donkey?" Hubbard asked.

She looked at him in absolute confusion.

"In Morocco," Hubbard said. "In the mountains, there's a little town called Ksar es Souk. There's a hotel there in what used to be a French Foreign Legion fort. Very good food, and what you do for recreation is get on donkeys and ride up into the mountains. An Arab holds the reins and trots along beside you. Ten minutes after you leave the hotel, you can't see anything green. And no matter how high you go up in the mountains, no matter how far you can see, you can't see any water. It's as if there is no water anywhere in the world."

She rested her head against his chest, and he felt her arms around his back.

"I think he'll like that," she said.

It probably isn't going to last, Hubbard thought. It might turn out to be an absolute disaster. But it would last for a while, anyway, and so long as it lasted, it would be good. Sometimes you just had to take the chance.

He heard the angry wasp sound of the little outboard on Tony Pombal's work boat. He looked out across the water and saw the boat headed toward the *Barbara-Ann*.

Laura pushed away from him and looked where he

was looking. He laid his hand gently on her shoulder and felt the warmth of her through the terrycloth blouse. She reached up and touched his hand and then laid her cheek against it.

Bestselling Books

☐ 21889-X	**EXPANDED UNIVERSE,** Robert A. Heinlein	$3.95
☐ 47809-3	**THE LEFT HAND OF DARKNESS,** Ursala K. LeGuin	$2.95
☐ 48519-7	**LIVE LONGER NOW,** Jon. N. Leonard, J. L. Hofer and N. Pritikin	$3.50
☐ 80581-7	**THIEVE'S WORLD,** Robert Lynn Asprin, Ed.	$2.95
☐ 02884-5	**ARCHANGEL,** Gerald Seymour	$3.50
☐ 08933-X	**BUSHIDO,** Beresford Osborne	$3.50
☐ 08950-X	**THE BUTCHER BOY,** Thomas Perry	$3.50
☐ 09231-4	**CASHING IN,** Antonia Gowar	$3.50
☐ 87127-5	**WALK ON GLASS,** Lisa Robinson	$3.50
☐ 78035-0	**STAR COLONY,** Keith Laumer	$2.95